m

LucyStone #5

VALENTINE MURDER

VALENTINE MURDER

A Lucy Stone Mystery

Leslie Meier

THORNDIKE
CHIVERS

This Large Print edition is published by Thorndike Press®,
Waterville, Maine USA and by BBC Audiobooks, Ltd,
Bath, England.

Published in 2004 in the U.S. by arrangement with
Kensington Books, an imprint of Kensington Publishing Corp.

Published in 2004 in the U.K. by arrangement with the author.

U.S. Hardcover 0-7862-6499-3 (Mystery)
U.K. Hardcover 1-4056-2999-1 (Chivers Large Print)
U.K. Softcover 1-4056-3000-0 (Camden Large Print)

The text of this Large Print edition is unabridged.
Other aspects of the book may vary from the original edition.

Set in 16 pt. Plantin by Minnie B. Raven.

Printed in the United States on permanent paper.

British Library Cataloguing-in-Publication Data available

Library of Congress Cataloging-in-Publication Data

Meier, Leslie.
   Valentine murder : a Lucy Stone mystery / Leslie Meier.
      p. cm.
   ISBN 0-7862-6499-3 (lg. print : hc : alk. paper)
   1. Stone, Lucy (Fictitious character) — Fiction.
   2. Women librarians — Crimes against — Fiction.
   3. Women detectives — Maine — Fiction.   4. Valentine's
Day — Fiction.   5. Women — Maine — Fiction.   6. Maine
— Fiction.   7. Large type books.   I. Title.
PS3563.E3455V35 2004
   813'.54—dc22   2004041279

VALENTINE MURDER

Prologue

Once upon a time there was a poor kitchen maid named Cinderella . . .

On the day she died, Bitsy Howell didn't want to get out of bed. Her bedroom was cold, for one thing. It was always cold, thanks to her landlady, Mrs. Withers, who turned the heat down to fifty-five degrees every night to save money on heating oil. It didn't matter one bit to Mrs. Withers that it was the coldest winter in twenty years.

And if the cold bedroom wasn't reason enough to stay in bed, well, the fact that it was Thursday made getting up especially difficult. Bitsy hated Thursdays.

Thursday was story hour day at the Broadbrooks Free Library where she was the librarian. Just thinking about story hour depressed Bitsy. She found it practically impossible to keep ten or fifteen preschool children focused on a storybook. Thanks to TV and video games, they had no attention span whatsoever. They fidgeted and wriggled in their seats, they picked their noses, they did everything except what Bitsy wanted them to do which was to sit quietly and listen to a nice story followed by a finger-play or song, or maybe a simple craft project.

This Thursday, however, happened to be the last Thursday in January. That meant the library's board of directors would meet, as they did on the third Thursday of every month. Bitsy would not only have to cope with story hour, but with the directors, too.

Bitsy had come to the tiny Broadbrooks Free Library in Tinker's Cove, Maine, from a big city library. One factor in her decision to leave had been her poor relationship with her boss, the head librarian. Little had she known that she was swapping one rather difficult menopausal supervisor for seven meddlesome and inquisitive directors.

Bitsy sighed and heaved herself out of bed. She padded barefoot around her rather messy bedroom, looking for her slippers. She found one underneath a magazine and the other tangled in a pair of sweat pants. One of these days, she promised herself, she would get organized and pick up the clothes that were strewn on the floor. Not today, of course. She didn't have time today.

On her way to the bathroom she raised the shade and peered out the window, blinking at the bright winter sunlight. Shit, she muttered. It had snowed again.

Arriving at the library, Bitsy studied the new addition which contained a children's room, workroom, and conference room. It was undeniably handsome, and badly needed, but it had been a dreadful bone of contention.

When she had first come to Tinker's Cove the library was a charming but antiquated old building that was far too small for the needs of the community. Getting the board to agree to build the addition, and then raising the money for it had been a struggle, one Bitsy wouldn't want to repeat. Now, if she could only get them to take the next step and buy some computers so the library could go on-line.

"Tiny baby steps," she muttered as she unlocked the door. Flicking on the lights as she went, Bitsy headed for her office. She had an hour or so before the library opened and she wanted to have her facts and figures straight before the board meeting.

Pushing aside a few of the papers that cluttered her desk, she set down a bag containing a Styrofoam cup of coffee, with cream and sugar, and a couple of sugary jelly doughnuts. She draped her coat over an extra chair and took her seat, flicking on the computer. Soon she was happily immersed in numbers and percentages, all the while slurping down her coffee and scattering powdered sugar all over her desk.

At ten minutes past ten she heard someone banging at the main entrance and realized she hadn't unlocked the doors.

"I'm so sorry," she apologized as she pulled open the heavy oak door. "I lost track of the time."

"No problem, my dear," said Gerald Asquith, smiling down at her benignly. Tall and gray-haired, dressed in a beautifully tailored cashmere overcoat, he was the retired president of Winchester College and one of the members of the board of directors. "I know I'm a bit early, but I want to go over the final figures for the addition before the meeting."

"Of course," said Bitsy. "I'll get the file for you."

Bitsy had hoped Gerald would seat himself at the big table in the reference room, but instead he hung his coat up on the rack by the door and followed her into her office. When she gave him the file he sat down at her desk, displacing her, and began studying it.

Bitsy gave a little shrug and headed for the children's section. She had to come up with something for story hour anyway; it was in less than an hour, at eleven.

She was leafing through a lavishly illustrated edition of *Cinderella* when she felt a presence behind her. Turning, she greeted Corney Clarke with a polite smile. Corney, an attractive blonde of indeterminate age, ran a busy catering service and called herself a "lifestyle consultant." She was also a member of the board of directors.

"Can I help you?" asked Bitsy, mindful of her status as an employee.

"No. I came a little early to see the new addition. It's a big improvement, isn't it?" said Corney, walking around the sunny area, admiring the low bookshelves and child-sized seating.

"It sure is," agreed Bitsy. "We must have been the only library in the state without a children's room."

"It must be fun doing story hour, now, in such nice surroundings," surmised Corney.

11

"Oh, yes," said Bitsy, attempting to sound enthusiastic. "Today we're reading *Cinderella*."

"Oh." Corney wrinkled her forehead in concern. "I don't want to tell you how to do your job, but are you sure that's a good choice?"

"The children like it . . ." began Bitsy.

"Well, of course they do. But does it send the right message?"

"It's just a fairy tale." Bitsy bit her lip. Personally, she didn't think every story had to have a socially redeeming message, and she wasn't sure Corney was the right person to decide what was suitable for young children, either. After all, she was childless and never married, though not from lack of effort.

"Well, we don't want our little girls growing up and thinking life is a fairy tale, do we? We don't want them to wait for Prince Charming to rescue them from the kitchen — we want them to become self-actualizing, don't we?" Corney gave Bitsy an encouraging smile, and patted her hand. "I'm sure you can find something more suitable." She paused for a moment and came up with a suggestion. "Like *The Little Engine that Could*," she said, turning and striding off in the direction of the office.

Bitsy rolled her eyes and replaced *Cinderella* on the shelf. Pulling out one volume after another, she dismissed them. Children's literature was so insipid these days. Everything had to have a positive, meaningful message. She wanted something with a little bite. Something exciting. She opened a battered copy of *Hansel and Gretel* and began turning the pages. This ought to keep the little demons' attention, she thought, admiring a lurid illustration of the tiny Hansel and Gretel cringing in terror as the grinning witch opened the oven door.

"Say, Bitsy, do you know where those figures for the addition are?"

Bitsy closed the book and turned to face Hayden Northcross, another member of the board of directors. Hayden was a small, neat man who was a partner in a prestigious antiques business that was known far beyond Tinker's Cove.

"Gerald's got them, in my office," said Bitsy.

"I'll see if he's through with them," said Hayden, turning to go. "Say, what's that?"

"*Hansel and Gretel*. For story hour."

"Oh, my dear! Not *Hansel and Gretel*!" exclaimed Hayden, throwing up his hands in horror.

"No? Why not?" inquired Bitsy, tightening her grip on the storybook and starting a slow mental count to ten.

"Not unless you want to traumatize the poor things," said Hayden. "I'll never forget how frightened I was when Mumsy read it to me. I think it may have affected my entire attitude toward women." He cocked an eyebrow and nodded meaningfully.

Bitsy wasn't quite sure how serious he was. Hayden and his business partner, Ralph Love, had also been domestic partners for years. Hayden thought it great fun to shock the more conservative residents of Tinker's Cove by flaunting his homosexuality.

"It's just a story," said Bitsy, defending her choice. "I'll be sure to remind them it's make-believe."

"I'm warning you. You're playing with fire," said Hayden, waggling his finger at her. "That book contains dangerous themes of desertion and cannibalism — the mothers are sure to object."

"You're probably right," said Bitsy, putting the book back on the shelf.

"You know I am," said Hayden, flashing her a smile. "See you at the meeting."

The meeting, thought Bitsy, biting her

14

lip. That was another sore point. The fact that the board met at the same time Bitsy was occupied with story hour was not co-incidental. She was convinced it was their way of letting her know she was not a decision maker. She was just the hired help, allowed to join the meeting only for the last half hour to give her monthly report.

It hadn't always been like that. When she first took the job, the board had sought her advice, and had adopted her suggestion that the library be expanded. But as time passed they seemed to grow less receptive to her views, and began easing her out of their meetings. They'd also become increasingly intrusive, always poking their noses into her work.

Bitsy checked her watch and resumed her search. She had better find something fast; it was already a quarter to eleven and little Sadie Orenstein had arrived. She was slowly slipping a big stack of books through the return slot in the circulation desk, one by one, while her mother studied the new books. The Orensteins were ferocious readers.

Pulling out book after book, she shook her head and shoved them back on the shelf. It seemed as if she had read them all, over and over. Absolutely nothing appealed until she found an old favorite, *Rumpelstiltskin*.

She smiled at the picture of the irate dwarf on the cover. The kids would like it, too, she thought. She would have them act it out and they could stamp their feet just like Rumpelstiltskin. Tucking the book under her arm, and telling Sadie she'd be right back, she hurried to the office. She'd just remembered that she had left a file open on the computer and wanted to close it.

There she found Ed Bumpus, yet another member of the board of directors, busy disassembling the copy machine. Ed was a big man and when he bent over the machine his shirt and pants parted, revealing rather more of his hairy backside than she wanted to see. She stared out the window at a snow-covered pine tree.

"We want copies of the addition finances for the meeting, but the danged machine won't work," explained Ed. He was a contractor and never hesitated to reach for a screwdriver.

"That's funny. It worked fine yesterday. Maybe it's out of paper. Or needs toner. Did you check?"

"What kind of idiot do you take me for? Of course I checked!" snapped Ed, growing a bit red under his plaid flannel shirt collar.

"We'll have to call for service, then," said Bitsy, leaning over Gerald to ease open her desk drawer. "You can make copies at the coin machine by the front desk. Here's the key."

"Could you be a doll and do it for me?" Ed gave her his version of an ingratiating smile.

Still leaning awkwardly over Gerald, Bitsy reached for the mouse and clicked it, closing the file. Then she took the report from Ed. More children had gathered for story hour — she could hear their voices. They would just have to wait a few minutes. She was not going to risk being insubordinate to one of the directors, especially Ed.

When she returned she found him lounging in the spare chair, sitting on top of her coat, and joking with Gerald, who was still sitting at her desk. What a pair, she thought, annoyed at the way they made themselves at home in her office.

"Here you go," she said, handing him the papers and turning to go. She really had to get story hour started.

"So you're reading *Rumpelstiltskin* to them today?" inquired Gerald, who was still sitting at her desk. His tone was friendly — he was just making conversation. Now that he was retired he had all the time in the world.

"I think they'll like it," said Bitsy, eager to get out to the children. Unsupervised, there was no telling what they might get up to.

"Well, I don't think it's a very good idea. It's a horrible story," said Ed. "It used to make my little girls cry."

"Really?" Bitsy kept her voice even. She was determined not to let him know how irritated she was.

"In fact, I don't even think it belongs in the library. With all the money we spend on new books I don't know why you're keeping a nasty old book like that. Just look at it — it's all worn out."

"I guess you're right," said Bitsy, who knew the acquisitions budget was a sore spot with Ed, who favored bricks and mortar over books. His objection, however, reminded her of a box of new material that had arrived the day before but hadn't been opened yet.

"I'm just going down to the workroom for a minute," she said, more to herself than the directors. Grabbing the box of art supplies and taking a pile of red construction paper from the corner of her desk, she quickly left the office and hurried through the children's room, giving the assembled mothers and children a cheerful wave.

"I'll be right with you — we're making Valentines today," she called, opening the door to the stairs that led to the lower level. She rushed down, hearing her footsteps echo in the poured concrete stairwell, but caught her foot on the rubber edging of the bottom step. She fell forward, twisting her ankle and bumping her head painfully on the doorknob. The sheets of red paper cascaded around her; the coffee can containing child-safe scissors clattered to the concrete floor and crayons rolled in every direction.

Groaning slightly, she pressed her hands to her forehead and sat down on the next to last step, waiting impatiently for the blinding agony to pass. Using a trick she'd picked up in a stress management workshop, she concentrated on her breathing, keeping her breaths even. Gradually, the pain receded. She unclenched her teeth and blinked her eyes. Grasping the handrailing, she pulled herself to her feet, only to feel a stabbing pain in her ankle. Conscious that she was already late for story hour, she tried putting her weight on it even though the pain made her wince. The ankle held and she limped through the dark and empty conference room and on into the brand new workroom. The workroom, unlike the conference room, had windows and she squinted her eyes against the bright sun. She bent over the box, which was sitting on the floor, and yanked at the tape.

Hearing the outside door open, she raised her head.

"Oh, it's *you*," she said, recognizing the figure outlined against the bright light streaming through the windows. Of all the nerve, she thought angrily. This was just too much; the morning was spinning out of control. She'd had enough. She took a deep breath, preparing to give vent to the emotions she had been suppressing for so long, but she never got the chance to say what was on her mind.

Bitsy Howell's last words were rudely interrupted.

One

*That country was ruled by a wise king
and his beautiful and kind queen . . .*

In the big kitchen of her restored farmhouse
on Red Top Road, Lucy Stone sang a little
song as she tucked the last of the breakfast
dishes into the dishwasher. She couldn't
help feeling cheerful. Today, after what
seemed like a solid month of cloudy skies
and snowstorms, the sun was finally shining.
The sky was a cloudless, bright blue. The
pine trees in the woods bordering the yard
were deep green, frosted with white.
Mounds of snow covered her car, the shed,
the garden fence; everything sparkled in the
sunlight. It was so bright that she had to
squint when she looked out the window.

Inside, it revealed crumbs and dust that
had gone unnoticed in the dim, cloud-
filtered daylight of recent weeks, along
with a few dried-out pine needles from the
Christmas tree. As the dishwasher

hummed she wiped off the counters with a sponge and straightened the mess of papers that had collected on the round golden oak table.

Looking at the now neat but ever-growing pile, she gave a big sigh. It was her "to-do" list. Bills to pay, car insurance renewal forms to file, bank statements to balance, income tax forms to complete. A partially completed feature story she was writing for the local paper, *The Pennysaver*. The latest issue of *Maine Library Journal*.

She glanced at the clock — it was a few minutes past eight. A peek in the family room revealed that her four-year-old daughter, Zoe, was happily playing a game on the family computer. She was the only one home besides Lucy. Lucy's husband, Bill, a restoration carpenter, was already at work. The older children were all in school: Toby, sixteen, and Elizabeth, fourteen, attended high school, and ten-year-old Sara was in third grade at the Tinker's Cove Elementary School.

No time like the present, decided Lucy, sitting down and picking up the magazine. The board meeting wasn't until eleven; she had plenty of time to read it and become familiar with library issues. It was her first meeting as a director and she wanted to make a good impression.

An hour later, her head was buzzing. What had she gotten herself into? Being a library director was a bigger responsibility than she thought. Budgets. Maintenance. Circulation. Employee relations. Acquisitions. Censorship. Information technology. Not to mention security.

She had no idea security was a big issue for libraries, but it was. Thanks to the journal she now knew that seven librarians in New England had been the victims of brutal attacks in the last year, and one had been raped. "Librarians, generally women, often work alone at night, so they are natural targets," explained the state library commissioner. "Libraries often contain valuable artifacts and rare books, not to mention an increasing amount of computer equipment. We have to be more vigilant about security, something we have tended to take for granted."

Poor Bitsy, thought Lucy, resolving to ask her fellow board members if the new addition had been equipped with an alarm system. If it hadn't been, it should, and the older part of the building should be included, too.

The dishwasher clicked off and Lucy checked the clock. Already past nine and

23

she wasn't dressed yet. Neither was Zoe, she realized.

"Come on, sweetie," called Lucy, standing in the doorway. "We have to get dressed. It's story hour day."

Zoe didn't move from the computer. Lucy repeated her request.

"Zoe, time to get dressed."

"I don't want to."

Surprised at this answer, Lucy crossed the room and peered over her daughter's shoulder at the brightly colored screen, where lime green robots were chasing a little brown bunny. "Is it a good game?" she asked.

Zoe didn't answer. Her attention was fixed on the screen; her chubby fingers were busy pushing buttons on the control pad.

"I'll tell you what," said Lucy, in a cheerful but firm voice. "You can play a little longer, while I get dressed. But then we'll have to turn off the computer. Okay?"

She looked expectantly at Zoe, waiting for an answer, and thought she detected a little nod. Good enough. She hurried upstairs, wondering exactly what a library director should wear.

Returning to the family room a half-hour later, Lucy was pleased with her choice.

She was wearing her good wool slacks, a turtleneck jersey, and the extravagantly expensive designer sweater Bill had given her for Christmas. She had added a simple gold chain and a pair of pearl earrings.

Now for the next challenge, she thought, surveying the family room where Zoe was still absorbed in "Bunny Beware". Another gift from Bill, but Lucy wasn't sure she approved of this one.

"Zoe, honey. Remember our bargain? Mommy's all dressed. Now it's your turn."

"I'm busy," said Zoe. The computer game had apparently rendered her immobile. Powerful electronic forces, emanating from the screen, had seized control of the little girl's mind and body. Something had to be done.

Lucy switched off the machine.

"Whaaaaaaa!" shrieked Zoe.

"It's time to get dressed," said Lucy. "You don't want to miss story hour, do you?"

"Story hour's dumb and Miss Howell's mean!"

"Zoe, that's enough," said Lucy, firmly taking her daughter's hand and leading her to the stairs. "What do you want to wear today? How about your turtleneck with the hearts? It's only two weeks 'til Valentine's Day, you know."

It was well after ten when Lucy and Zoe, bundled against the single-digit weather in bulky down parkas and snow boots, left the house. Bill and Toby had shoveled a path to the driveway earlier that morning, but they hadn't cleared the snow off the car. With a gloved hand Lucy scraped the snow away from the door handle and pulled. It didn't budge. It was frozen shut by a layer of ice that had formed underneath the snow.

"This is going to take a while," Lucy told Zoe. "Why don't you make some snow angels for Mommy?"

It was a quarter to eleven when Lucy and Zoe finally got underway in the old Subaru station wagon. Thank goodness for four wheel drive, thought Lucy, as they made steady but slow progress over the snow-covered roads. In Tinker's Cove the DPW plowed, but set the blades high, leaving an inch or two of snow to protect the expensive asphalt.

If you didn't like snow, thought Lucy, you shouldn't live in Maine. At least not this winter with record low temperatures and unusually heavy snowfalls. Fortunately, she loved cold weather and always felt a sense of excitement when the flakes began to fall. As she drove along, she was enchanted by the way last night's storm had turned the bare winter trees into a glistening fairyland.

Turning onto Main Street, she thought that Tinker's Cove, with its red brick storefronts and tall-steepled white church, was truly a picture-perfect New England town. Today, however, Main Street seemed deserted; few people were out and about in the bitter cold. She spotted Mr. Ericson, the postman, bundled up in a red and black buffalo plaid jacket and a checked wool cap with black fur earflaps. She gave the horn a friendly toot as she passed him.

Turning into the library parking lot, she saw there were a number of cars. No wonder, she thought; she was late. It was already ten past eleven. Story hour was bound to attract a crowd of mothers and kids tired of being cooped up at home. The directors would also have gathered for their meeting. She parked the car and helped Zoe out of her seatbelt and booster seat and they hurried up the narrow path between the snowbanks.

"We're late, we're late," she began.

"For an important date!" exclaimed Zoe,

completing the rhyme and stamping her purple Barbie boots on the cocoa fiber mat.

"For my first meeting," fretted Lucy, as she pulled open the door.

Two

When Snow White awakened from her nap, she was surprised to see the Seven Dwarves . . .

As they entered the library, Lucy's eyes were drawn as always to the softly gleaming pewter tankard that sat in a locked display case in the entry. A neatly printed label identified it as "Josiah's Tankard" and noted it had been presented to the library in 1887 by Henry Hopkins, the last surviving descendent of Josiah Hopkins, who was the first European to settle in Tinker's Cove. The tankard, which had been handed down through the family, was said to have been brought from England by Josiah.

If one looked closely, and the light was right, an elaborate design featuring a flowering shrub with a bird perched on one of the branches could still be discerned in the tankard's worn and battered surface. The initials "J" and "H" were somewhat easier to see, along with the date, 1698.

Lucy thought the library was a fitting place for the tankard, which represented the long history of the little town that was first incorporated in 1703. Whatever drew Josiah Hopkins to this rugged spot on the Maine coast was a puzzle, considering the brutally cold winters and the stony soil unfit for farming, but the homestead he built had stood until just a few years ago when it had burned to the ground in a spectacular fire that had claimed the life of Lucy's friend, Monica Mayes.

The homestead was gone, but the tankard had survived, safe in the library. Lucy found that comforting, just as she believed it was a privilege to live in a house that had sheltered many generations before her family had moved in. Living in a place that had ties to the past gave her a sense of security; she liked knowing that she was yet another link in a long chain of mothers and fathers and children connecting the unknowable future to the past.

Today, however, Lucy and Zoe didn't have time to admire the tankard. Instead, they pushed open the second set of doors and greeted Miss Tilley, who was seated at the circulation desk.

"I see they've put you back to work," said Lucy.

Miss Tilley had been the librarian for years, until she retired and Bitsy took her place. With her white hair and china blue eyes, Miss Tilley looked like the very image of a sweet old lady. Lucy knew better, and enjoyed her old friend's tart wit and sharp tongue.

"There should be a volunteer on duty, considering that Bitsy has story hour today, but nobody has shown up yet," said Miss Tilley, who only allowed her very dearest friends to call her by her first name, Julia. She was holding the "Date Due" stamp as if she couldn't wait to use it.

Lucy knelt to unfasten Zoe's pink parka, and gave her a little pat in the direction of the children's room. "See you later, sweetie," she said, watching as Zoe went to join her friends.

"We never had these problems when I was in charge," said Miss Tilley, leaning forward and whispering loudly to Lucy. "The volunteers knew that they were expected to come on their assigned days."

"Well, Bitsy has had a lot on her mind with the new addition and all." Lucy looked around, noting how well the new construction meshed with the older portions of the building. "It looks great, doesn't it?"

"Hummph," snorted Miss Tilley. "I just hope the heating bill doesn't bankrupt us."

"I doubt it will. Nowadays they use lots of insulation." Lucy looked around. "So where does the board meet?" she asked.

"We've always used the reference room, but I expect that will change now that we have that conference room. Why they put it in the cellar is something I'll never understand. Cellars are for storage — they're not fit for human habitation."

"Is that where everyone is?" asked Lucy, smiling at Miss Tilley's stubborn resistance to change.

"Not yet. I think they're still in Bitsy's office," said Miss Tilley, taking a pile of books that a young mother was returning. "That will be seventy-five cents," she said, sounding awfully pleased to have caught the overdue books.

Lucy went around the desk and down the dark little hallway leading to Bitsy's office. She smoothed her sweater nervously and took a deep breath, then pushed open the door.

"If it isn't our newest member," exclaimed Gerald Asquith, greeting her warmly. "Welcome! Everybody — this is Lucy Stone, who's made quite a little reputation for herself as a writer for our local newspaper, *The Pennysaver.*"

"A very little reputation," said Lucy, blushing. She enjoyed freelance writing for the paper, but was rarely able to manage more than one or two feature stories a month.

"I'm Ed Bumpus," said Ed, leaning forward in his chair to shake her hand. "I know your husband, Bill. We're in the same business."

"I've heard him speak of you," said Lucy, giving him a friendly smile. She looked around at the others, searching for familiar faces. "I know Corney, of course, but you probably don't remember me. I've attended some of your workshops. I enjoyed them very much."

Lucy extended her hand but Corney ignored it, merely nodding vacantly and murmuring, "Oh, yes."

"Hayden Northcross, here," said Hayden, promptly filling the void and taking Lucy's hand with both of his. "I must say it's nice to have some new blood on the board."

"I guess we're all here then, except for Chuck," said Ed. Lucy couldn't decide if he was grumbling, or if his voice always sounded that gruff.

"You know he tends to run late," said

Corney, leaping to the absent member's defense. "After all, he's a lawyer. He'll be here."

"It's well after eleven — shall we go down?" suggested Gerald.

There was a murmur of assent, and the directors began moving toward the door.

"You know, Bitsy seems to have less and less control over those children every week," said Corney, hearing the noise from the children's room.

"She's not there," said Lucy, observing the group of lively pre-schoolers and a handful of chatting mothers. "Where could she be?"

"I think she said she was going down to the workroom," offered Gerald.

"Maybe she's lost track of the time. I'll run ahead and remind her," volunteered Lucy, eager to be helpful.

"Young legs," said Gerald, nodding approvingly as Lucy headed in the direction of the stairway.

"I'll see if Miss Tilley's free," said Corney, as if to remind everyone that she used to be the youngest person on the board and, even though she now had to share that distinction, was still no older than Lucy.

Corney was just approaching the circulation desk when Chuck Canaday made his appearance, bursting through the doors with his unbuttoned coat flapping about him, bringing a wave of cold air.

"Ooh — it's cold out there," said Corney, wrapping her arms across her chest and greeting him with a smile.

"It's invigorating," said Chuck, giving his thick mop of gray hair a shake. "Makes me wish I had more time for skiing."

"Me, too," agreed Corney. "I had a great time at Brewster Mountain last weekend."

"Really? How was the snow?"

"Fresh powder."

"Uh-hmm." Miss Tilley interrupted their little exchange. "Everyone's waiting for us. It's time we joined the meeting."

"Who'll watch the desk?" asked Corney.

"Bitsy will have to do it — there's no one else," said Miss Tilley. "It's not very busy, and she can leave story hour if the need arises."

Chuck and Corney's eyes met; Corney gave a little shrug, and they followed Miss Tilley toward the waiting group.

Having left the others at the office, Lucy hurried across the children's room where she was happy to see that Zoe was busy chatting with her friend, Sadie Orenstein.

Whatever do four-year-olds talk about? she wondered, as she pulled open the steel door to the stairs. As she thumped down in her snow boots she noticed the mess of paper and art supplies spilled at the foot of the stairs, and quickly picked them up, wondering what had happened. She set the box down in the corner and pulled open the door to the conference room, flicking on the lights.

"Bitsy?" she called. "Are you down here?"

Receiving no answer, Lucy went on through to the workroom door. She gave a little knock and pulled it open.

It took a moment or two for her to register the sight: Bitsy was lying flat on her back, legs and arms awkwardly akimbo, like one of Zoe's discarded dolls.

"Oh, my God," exclaimed Lucy, rushing toward her. She bent over the fallen woman, noticing her eyes were wide open and there was an odd look of surprise on her face. Lucy instinctively stepped back, and saw a hole in Bitsy's cardigan sweater, just above her heart. It was then she noticed the puddle of blood seeping beneath Bitsy's body.

Repulsed, Lucy forced herself to search for a pulse and reached for Bitsy's wrist with trembling hands, hoping to find a flutter of life. Her arm felt heavy, like a dead weight, and Lucy knew it was futile. It was obvious Bitsy was dead.

Lucy's heart was racing and she felt dizzy and sick to her stomach as she backed away from the body. This was no longer Bitsy; this was something horrifying and frightening. She was shaking all over, and her teeth were chattering. She had only one thought: she had to get away. She turned and fled, running out of the workroom, across the conference room, and up the stairs. Throwing open the door, she ran smack into the group of directors. Suddenly speechless, her mouth made a noiseless little "O".

Three

The Gingerbread Man was afraid to cross the stream, but along came a clever fox . . .

"What's the matter?" asked Gerald, taking her hands in his.

"It's B-b-b," said Lucy, her eyes darting wildly at the group clustered around her. Their faces seemed distorted, as if they were reflections in a convex mirror. She suddenly felt woozy and the room began to whirl around her.

"Lucy, get a grip on yourself," scolded Miss Tilley.

She turned toward the voice, and her eyes settled on her old friend. Then, looking beyond the group, she saw the mothers and children waiting for story hour to begin. She watched as Zoe settled beside Sadie and opened a book for them to look at together. It was all so normal, so peaceful. Nothing like the awful thing downstairs.

"Is Bitsy hurt? Has she fallen?" Gerald peered over her shoulder, at the stairs.

Lucy straightened her back and took a deep breath. "She's dead."

"That can't be," insisted Miss Tilley.

"There must be some mistake," added Corney.

"I'd better take a look," said Ed, stepping to the front of the group.

"I don't think you should," protested Lucy, as the group surged past her and hurried down the stairs. "At least not until the police get here," she added, leaning against the wall for support. She was still dizzy and trembling with shock.

The police, she thought. I've got to call the police. But she found herself hesitating, reluctant to move. Instead, she watched Zoe, who was pointing at something in the book. It must be funny — the two little girls were giggling.

Somewhat shaky on her feet, Lucy stepped away from the wall, determined to get control of herself. Now that she was back upstairs in the sunny new addition, she could hardly believe what she had seen in the basement. She felt a little surge of hope. Maybe she'd been wrong. Maybe it wasn't too late for Bitsy. The rescue squad had defibrillators and all kinds of life-saving equipment.

Walking carefully so as not to alarm the mothers and children, she went to the office. There she picked up the receiver and, using all her concentration, punched in 9-1-1 with a trembling hand.

"Tinker's Cove Rescue. This is a recorded line."

"There's a . . . we need help . . . fast. No, I think it's . . ." stammered Lucy, furious at herself because she still couldn't seem to form a simple sentence.

"Take it easy," said the dispatcher, trained to handle emergencies. "What's your name?"

"Lucy Stone."

"Where are you, Lucy?"

"The library."

"What's the problem?"

"Bitsy Howell — I think she's been shot."

"I'm sending an ambulance and I'm notifying the police. Have you been trained in CPR?"

"I can't," said Lucy, thinking of Bitsy's bloody body.

"That's all right," said the dispatcher. "Just stay calm. Help will be there in a few minutes."

"I can already hear the sirens," said

Lucy, remembering that the police and rescue station was just around the corner from the library.

"Can you open the doors? Make sure they can get in?" asked the dispatcher.

"I can do that," said Lucy, who had clung to the dispatcher's calm voice like a lifeline. "Thank you."

She went to the front door and hailed the paramedics, who were stepping out of the ambulance. She held the door open for them and they hurried in, carrying cases of equipment. Lucy pointed them to the stairs.

As they rushed through the children's room the mothers and children looked up in surprise.

Oh, dear, thought Lucy. I'll have to give them some sort of explanation. She crossed the circulation area and leaned against one of the low children's bookcases for support.

"We've had an accident. There won't be any story hour today. I think we'll have to close the library."

"What is it?" asked Juanita Orenstein, Sadie's mother. "Can I help?"

The others looked at Lucy expectantly, curious about the sudden change in plans.

"I think it would be best if everyone just

left," said Lucy, thinking of the children.

"That's too bad," said Anne Wilson, who was firmly holding each of her three-year-old twin boys by the hand. "We'll have to wait 'til next week, fellas."

"That's right, come back next week," Lucy told the mothers, who began gathering up their belongings and zipping their children into snowsuits.

"Lucy, you look terrible," said Juanita, wrapping an arm around her shoulder. "What's going on?"

"Bitsy's badly hurt," Lucy whispered.

"Oh, no!" Juanita's big brown eyes were full of concern. "What happened?"

"I'm not sure." Lucy was already regretting giving in to the impulse to confide in Juanita and arousing her curiosity. "Could you do me a favor and take Zoe home with you? I don't know how long I'm going to have to stay here."

"Sure," said Juanita. "Take as long as you need — I don't have any plans for today."

"Thanks," said Lucy. "I really appreciate it." She went over to Zoe and Sadie in the corner. "Guess what? You're going to have lunch at Sadie's today," she told Zoe.

The girls turned to face each other, and they raised their eyebrows in happy surprise before dissolving into giggles.

"Let me know if there's anything else I can do," offered Juanita, zipping up her jacket.

"Thanks," said Lucy, watching as the mothers and children began leaving.

She wondered if she ought to have some record of who was present at the library, so she went over to the circulation desk and found a piece of paper.

"Before you go, would you mind putting your names down here?" she asked, as the group started to file past the desk. When everyone was gone she took out a second sheet of paper, wrote "Library Closed Today" on it, and went outside to tape it to the door. The cold made her shiver, and her teeth began chattering. She hurried back inside, automatically glancing at the tankard. Only when she saw it was still safe in its locked case did she think to wonder if Bitsy had been shot because she interrupted a robbery. She was about to lock the door, when she heard someone pounding up the granite steps outside. She opened the door a crack and saw Officer Barney Culpepper.

Barney was a big man with a face like a Saint Bernard and a belly that hung over his belt. Lucy thought she'd never been so glad to see anyone. Barney was an old friend ever since the days when she'd been a Cub Scout den mother and they'd served together on the pack committee.

"What in heck's goin' on here, Lucy?" he asked, wiping his size thirteen boots on the mat and removing his hat.

"I think Bitsy was shot." Even as she said it she could hardly believe it.

Barney's eyes widened in surprise, but otherwise he remained as unflappable as ever.

"I guess I better see for myself. Where is she?"

"Downstairs."

She started to follow him, but decided against it. She couldn't face seeing Bitsy's body again. She took a seat instead and looked around the empty library, trying to think if there was anything else she should be doing. A minute or two later the board members began returning to the upper level, apparently on Barney's orders.

"Who does he think he is?" fumed an indignant Corney. "I've never been spoken to in that tone by anyone!"

"He's right," said Chuck. "We should never have gone down there. We may have destroyed important evidence."

"We didn't know that," said Hayden.

44

"She could have been hurt and needed help."

"The poor woman is past help now," said Gerald. He sat down opposite Lucy, on one of the child-sized seats. He looked pale and shaken.

"Barney Culpepper — I remember when you were a little boy with dirty hands. Don't think you can tell me what to do!" Miss Tilley burst through the door, with Culpepper close on her heels.

"I'm sorry, Miss Tilley. I'm just doing my job. Now I want you to sit down and wait. When the state police get here I'm sure they'll have some questions for you." He paused and surveyed the group. "That goes for all of you. Just make yourselves as comfortable as you can."

"This isn't very comfortable," said Gerald, rising stiffly to his feet. "I propose we all move to the conference room."

"No can do," said Barney, shaking his head and planting himself in the doorway. "Nobody goes downstairs."

"The reference room," suggested Miss Tilley, leading the way.

The other board members followed her and seated themselves in the captain's chairs at the big table in the center of the paneled room. From his perch above the fireplace, an abundantly whiskered Henry Hopkins looked out from his portrait with his usual expression of smug satisfaction.

"What do we do now?" asked Gerald, who was president of the board. He looked toward Chuck, naturally relying on his legal expertise. "Is there some action we should take as a board?"

"Not yet," replied Chuck. "All we can do is wait for whoever will be in charge of the investigation to get here." He paused and shook his shaggy head slowly. "I can't believe this."

"It's terrible," said Hayden, his face still white with shock.

"We may have to close the library for a while," said Chuck, scratching his chin thoughtfully. "It's a crime scene, after all. The police may insist."

"Crime scene? Couldn't it have been an accident?" asked Hayden, fidgeting nervously with his watchband.

"She was shot! Any idiot could see that!" thundered Ed, regarding Hayden with a scowl. Lucy suspected he didn't much like Hayden under the best of circumstances.

"Shot? I didn't hear a shot," insisted Hayden.

"Who could hear anything? Those kids were making such a racket," said Corney.

46

She seemed rather put out at this unexpected turn of events.

"I can't believe it," said Lucy, echoing Chuck. "Just this morning I was reading that seven librarians were attacked since last July. Now it's eight."

"I read the same article," offered Chuck. "It said libraries are targeted because of the computers and other valuables."

"The tankard!" exclaimed Miss Tilley. A bright red splotch appeared on each of her crepey cheeks.

"It's all right," said Lucy, hastening to reassure the old woman. "It hasn't been touched."

"I guess that means we can rule out theft as the motive," observed Gerald.

"Maybe it was something personal," offered Corney. "A boyfriend, maybe."

"I wouldn't doubt it," sniffed Miss Tilley. "These girls today just beg for trouble."

"Poor Bitsy," sighed Hayden. "Somehow she seems a very unlikely victim."

"What's that supposed to mean?" challenged Ed.

It was like a reflex, thought Lucy, becoming interested in the dynamics between the board members. If Hayden spoke, Ed had to respond negatively.

"I just can't imagine why anyone would want to kill her," mused Hayden, undeterred by Ed's hostility. He sighed. "Poor Bitsy."

"I can't help but wish this had happened someplace else," said Gerald, drumming his fingers on the table. "I mean, it shouldn't have happened at all, of course, but why did it have to happen here?"

"If you want my opinion, it seems all too typical," said Corney. "We might as well admit it: Bitsy was disorganized. Her office was a disgrace — papers and dirty cups everywhere. She was so messy it's a wonder she got anything done." Corney shook her head. "Her life was probably a mess, too."

"She sure was messy," agreed Ed.

"She ran the library very poorly," sniffed Miss Tilley. "The volunteers weren't properly organized, the new acquisitions were not shelved promptly, she was always late with circulation figures — I could just go on and on. In fact, I was planning to give her a very poor evaluation."

Listening to the others, Lucy was shocked. The woman was dead, after all. Truth be told, if she had been killed by an intruder as Lucy suspected, they all had to bear some responsibility. As the library's board of directors, they were her employers.

"Well, hell," said Chuck, slamming his fist down hard on the table. "I liked Bitsy and I think this is a damned shame. She had her faults — we all do, for that matter — but she didn't deserve to die. She was just doing her job the best she could and now she's dead." He pulled out a handkerchief and blew his nose noisily. "All I can say is I hope they catch the bastard who did this!"

"I certainly intend to."

They all turned in surprise to look at a slight, pale man with a long upper lip, rather like a rabbit, who was standing in the doorway.

"Let me introduce myself. I'm Detective Lieutenant Horowitz. I'm with the state police, and I'm in charge of the investigation." He paused, studying the group. "So, who wants to go first?"

Four

"Gingerbread Man, climb on my back and I will carry you safely across the stream," said the clever fox.

"As president of the library, I suppose that honor falls to me," said Gerald. He glanced at Chuck in a silent plea for support and received a little nod. "What do you want to know?"

"Let's start with the introductions," said Horowitz, pulling a notebook out of his pocket. As Gerald named each member of the board, Horowitz made a notation in the book, jotting down that person's address and phone number.

Lucy wondered if Horowitz would acknowledge her; after all, she first met the state police detective years before when she had been working at Country Cousins, the giant catalog retailer, and discovered the owner, Sam Miller, dead in his car. When her turn came, however, he didn't show the slightest flicker of recognition and treated her exactly like the others. Maybe her appearance had changed, she thought. After all, she wasn't getting any younger.

When Horowitz had finished getting all the names he looked up from his notebook and studied the group, letting his gaze rest on each of the directors. As he studied them, Lucy noticed a slight shifting of chairs, as if the individual members were joining together to present a united front against this outsider. Their reaction made her feel oddly isolated. She wasn't really part of the group yet, and after hearing them talk about Bitsy, she wasn't sure she wanted to be. Finally, Horowitz spoke.

"Let's go through the events of the morning — who got here first?"

"That would be Bitsy," said Gerald. "The victim."

"When was that?"

"I'm not absolutely certain of the time, but she was supposed to begin work at nine. I arrived at ten, when the library is due to open, and found the doors locked. I knocked and she let me in. She said she had been working and forgot the time."

"If the library doesn't open until ten,

51

why did she come in at nine?" asked Horowitz.

"To prepare for the day, to do paperwork, that sort of thing," said Gerald.

"What was she doing when you arrived?"

"Something at the computer, I think," said Gerald. "It was on when I came in but the screensaver program had started. Flying toasters or some such nonsense."

Horowitz consulted his notebook. "And you were here for a meeting?"

"That's right. We're all members of the board of directors."

"And what time was the meeting supposed to start?"

"At eleven," said Gerald.

Horowitz looked sharply at Gerald. "You came an hour early? What for?"

Gerald looked a bit uncomfortable. "Well, I wanted to go over the agenda."

"Anything special on that agenda?"

"Not really. Everything was pretty much routine." He paused and studied his hands. "We had received the contractor's final bill for the new addition and needed to authorize the last payment. That was the only new business."

"Any problems about that?"

Gerald waved a hand in the direction of the new children's room. "I think the addition pretty much speaks for itself — everyone's delighted."

A small "hmmph" of dissent could be heard from Miss Tilley's corner of the table, but everyone else nodded agreement, eager to show support for their leader.

"Any conflicts among the board members? Problems with Bitsy?"

"Oh, no," said Gerald. He couldn't resist glancing furtively toward Chuck, who gave him the slightest nod.

"All one big, happy family?" asked Horowitz.

"Absolutely," said Gerald, his voice a bit too loud.

Horowitz nodded. "Okay — who came next?"

"I guess that would be me," said Corney, who had prepared her explanation. "I came early because I wanted to see the furniture in the new addition."

"And what time was that?"

"Let me see," said Corney, producing a leather agenda and opening it. She ran down a list of things to do with a neatly manicured finger. "I stopped at the post office and the florist shop on the way, oh, and I stopped in at the garage to make an appointment to have my tires rotated. It must have been about ten-fifteen when I got here."

"Thank you," said Horowitz with a tired little sigh. "What did you do when you arrived?"

"Well, first I took off my boots and put on my shoes — I do so hate to track snow onto the carpeting. It's really bad for the fibers and it's no bother to bring shoes if you have an attractive tote. They're available in a variety of fabrics and coordinate with almost any outfit."

Lucy was suddenly self-conscious about her snow boots, which she hadn't thought to remove, and was glad they were hidden beneath the table.

"And then I hung up my coat in the closet," continued Corney, who seemed determined to turn every answer into a lifestyle lecture. "Good clothing is an investment, you know, and it lasts so much longer if you take proper care of it. After that I went to see the new children's room and I chatted a bit with Bitsy. I looked around some more and then I joined the others in the office. Maybe it was ten-thirty or so."

"What was Bitsy doing then?"

"I believe she was choosing a book for story hour," said Corney.

"When is story hour?"

"At eleven."

"The same time as the meeting?" Horowitz sounded doubtful. "Isn't that kind of unusual?"

"Not at all," said Miss Tilley, eager to clear up the confusion. "As directors, we felt our valuable paid staff was better employed elsewhere during meetings. We wished to avoid any duplication of effort."

Horowitz shook his head and frowned. "Wouldn't it be more usual to include her — for input?"

"We found Bitsy's input most valuable," said Chuck. "She always came for the last half-hour or so, after story hour, to give a report and answer questions."

"I see," said Horowitz, dropping the matter. "Okay — let's summarize. It's ten-thirty. Mr. Asquith is in the office, and the victim is in the children's room with Ms. Clarke. Is anybody else here?"

"I was," said Hayden. "When I arrived I saw Corney and Bitsy talking." He nodded nervously. "I went to join them but Corney had wandered off, so I spoke with Bitsy."

"What did you talk about?"

Hayden shrugged. "Books. Nothing of consequence."

"All right," said Horowitz impatiently.

"How long did you talk about nothing with the victim?"

"A few minutes. Then I asked her about the addition figures. She told me Gerald had them in the office and I went there."

Horowitz narrowed his lashless eyelids. "You were concerned about these figures?"

"Not at all," Hayden hastened to assure him. "Just curious. This was a big project and I wanted to know if it came in under budget."

"Did it?"

"You're darn tootin' it did," said Ed, leaning back in his chair and propping one ankle on his knee. "If Ed Bumpus says it's gonna cost so much, that's how much it costs."

"You were the contractor?" Horowitz raised his pale eyebrows.

"Not for this job, no. But I've got the experience and I took charge of things for the board. Made sure it got done right. And under budget."

"And what time did you arrive this morning?"

"Lemme see — I guess around ten-thirty. Maybe later. I saw him," he stabbed a finger toward Hayden, "talking with Bitsy when I came in. I went straight to the office, to make copies for the meeting.

Danged machine didn't work."

"When you got to the office, who was there?"

"Just him," said Ed, pointing to Gerald with a thick finger. "Nobody could get the machine to work, so when Bitsy came she went off to the front to make the copies on the coin machine. That's when he came in and her, too," he said, pointing to Hayden and Corney.

"That's right," said Miss Tilley in a clear, precise tone. "I came as I always do at a quarter to eleven. The volunteer responsible for the circulation desk had not shown up, something that unfortunately is not all that unusual. I noticed that quite a few books had been returned, and someone was waiting to check one out, so I took charge temporarily. While I was at the desk two directors came in — Lucy and Chuck." Miss Tilley clucked her tongue. "They were both late."

"I was late," admitted Lucy, with an apologetic little smile. "It was ten past when I arrived. I greeted Miss Tilley, sent my daughter over to the children's section for story hour, and went into the office to join the others. They were ready to begin the meeting, but Bitsy hadn't started story hour, so I went downstairs to get her."

Horowitz held up his hand. "Whoa. When did Bitsy go downstairs? And why?"

"It must have been close to eleven by then," said Gerald, looking to the other board members for confirmation.

"I think that's right," agreed Corney.

"And why did she go downstairs?"

"To get something, I guess," said Ed, scratching his chin. "She kinda ran off."

"As if she'd just remembered something?" asked Horowitz.

"Yeah," said Ed.

"Let me get this straight, now," said Horowitz. "Mrs. Stone went downstairs to get Bitsy sometime after eleven-ten. Where are the rest of you?"

"Well, we were leaving the office, on our way to the conference room," said Gerald.

"All of you together? As a group?"

"No. I went to the front to get Miss Tilley," said Corney. "That's when Chuck arrived."

"Okay. Mr. Canaday, Miss Tilley, and Ms. Clarke are in the front by the desk. Mr. Northcross, Mr. Asquith, and Mr. Bumpus are leaving the office. Mrs. Stone is downstairs. Is that right?"

They all nodded.

"And all this time nobody was alone?

You were all in each other's company all the time?"

The directors exchanged uneasy glances.

"There was quite a bit of coming and going," admitted Corney, looking around the table. "I certainly couldn't say that for sure."

"I admit it — I made a pit stop," said Ed. Seeing Horowitz's puzzled expression he added, "You know — the men's room."

Horowitz nodded.

"And I went into the reference room," added Gerald. "I went to get the gavel. It's stored in a closet there."

"Before this goes any further I'd like to know what you're getting at," said Chuck. "You seem awfully interested in our movements. Is one of the directors under suspicion?"

"At this point of the investigation everybody's a suspect," said Horowitz.

"That's ridiculous!" exclaimed Gerald. "None of us killed Bitsy. It must have been someone from outside — the workroom has an outside door, you know."

"I know," said Horowitz. "That was one of the first things I checked."

"And?" inquired Chuck, taking over from Gerald.

"Nobody came in that way."

"How can you be so sure?"

"It was locked."

"Of course," agreed Chuck, nodding thoughtfully.

The directors avoided each others' eyes, and carefully studied the small section of table directly in front of each of them while Horowitz went on.

"Whoever killed her either came in through the main door — or had a key to the outside workroom door."

Lucy felt the room begin to swirl around her as the image of Bitsy's body came back to her. She tightened her grip on the arms of her chair.

"That doesn't mean one of us did it. The library's a public building. Anyone can come in," said Gerald.

"That's true," said Horowitz. "Did you see anyone who seemed suspicious?"

"No," volunteered Lucy. "The only people here besides us were the mothers and children for story hour." She paused and added helpfully, "I had them all write down their names before they left."

"Did any of you see anyone else?" asked Horowitz.

The directors shifted uneasily and shook their heads.

"Just because we didn't see anyone

60

doesn't mean that someone didn't come in," insisted Chuck. "Perhaps someone who had a personal score to settle. And with all these bookshelves, it would be easy for someone to remain unnoticed."

Horowitz nodded. "I'll keep that in mind. Thank you all for your cooperation. I know it's past lunchtime and you must be hungry. You're free to go now, but I'd like you all to remain available to assist in the investigation."

"What does that mean?" asked Hayden.

"It means don't leave town," said Ed. "Right?"

"Not quite," said Horowitz. "If you plan to go on vacation in the near future, please let me know. That's all."

There was an audible sigh of relief from the board members when Horowitz turned to leave, pausing in the doorway to consult with a uniformed trooper.

"Well, this is quite a new experience," said Corney, turning her big blue eyes on Chuck. "I've never been a suspect before."

"I can't believe he really thinks one of us did it," protested Hayden. "It's absurd."

"Well, I don't think he could suspect me," said Lucy. "After all, I found Bitsy."

There was a murmur of sympathy from the board members, and Hayden reached across the table and gave her hand a little squeeze.

"By the way, Mrs. Stone," said Horowitz, turning to face the group. "I ought to mention that you will be of particular interest to the investigators."

"Me?" squeaked Lucy. "Why?"

"Precisely because you found the body." He paused. "Studies show that the person who reports a murder quite often turns out to be the murderer. You found the body, you made the call — that makes you the prime suspect."

Five

There was an old woman who lived in a shoe,
She had so many children
she didn't know what to do.

"What?" exclaimed Lucy, jumping to her feet and following Horowitz out of the reference room. She was slightly out of breath when she caught up with him by the circulation desk. "You don't really think I killed Bitsy, do you?" she asked. "You know who I am, don't you? Don't you remember me?"

Horowitz took his time answering. "I remember you, all right," he said, tilting his head and studying her with his pale eyes. "And I think we ought to get one thing straight right from the start: I don't want you playing detective. Got it?"

"I have no intention of doing any such thing," Lucy announced indignantly. "And why did you say I was the prime suspect, in front of everybody?"

"Just stirring the pot a bit," he said,

scratching his chin thoughtfully as he watched the directors beginning to leave. Miss Tilley was the first to go, leaning on Hayden's arm. "So tell me, was anything they said in there the truth?"

"Don't ask me," said Lucy with a toss of her head. "I'm not supposed to play detective, remember? Besides, I'm new. Today was my first meeting."

"Some first meeting," said Horowitz with a sardonic little grin. Out of the corner of his eye he was watching Ed Bumpus, who was apparently disagreeing with Chuck about something.

"It was awful." Lucy looked down at the floor, then raised her eyes to meet Horowitz's. "I can't believe anybody would want to kill Bitsy. She was nice to everybody. She was always willing to help you find things. She sure changed the atmosphere in the library — not that Miss Tilley wasn't wonderful in her own way. But Bitsy made it a fun place to be. I came in at least once a week. She had all the new books, and you always ran into somebody you knew."

"Well, somebody sure didn't like her," he said. "And they did a pretty neat job of killing her."

"Were you really serious when you said it

was one of the directors?"

Just then Lucy heard the door slam, and looked up to see that Ed had left and Chuck was deep in conversation with Gerald. Corney was standing a little apart, probably waiting for Chuck.

"Seems likely."

"Well, if that's so, why didn't you question us individually? And why didn't you check our hands? I thought there's some chemical test that tells if you've fired a gun."

"There is," said Horowitz with a long sigh, "but I don't think your good buddy Canaday was going to let me administer paraffin tests to the board members, do you? First thing he'd do is give a little speech about how everybody wants to cooperate with the investigation, but of course, they also need to protect their rights, so they'll be happy to cooperate after they've retained legal counsel. I'm not going to be able to get anything from that crew, believe me."

"I really think I could be helpful," offered Lucy. "Maybe they'd talk to me since I'm a member of the board."

"Oh, no," said Horowitz, holding up his hands. "The way you can help is by minding your own business and leaving the investigation to the experts."

His gaze shifted and Lucy turned to see Chuck approaching them; Gerald and Corney had left.

"Lucy, I don't think we've been formally introduced. I'm Chuck Canaday." He reached out his hand to shake hers.

"It wasn't much of a morning for formalities," said Lucy, taking his hand. "Of course I know who you are. I've seen you around town."

"Same here, and I've heard nothing but good things about you. I'm glad you've joined the board." He paused and gave her a half smile. "Our meetings are usually a lot quieter — you had a terrible shock this morning. I really think you ought to go home now and get some rest. And just for your information, Gerald has asked me to represent the board in the investigation," he said, giving Horowitz a pointed look, "but if you wish to retain your own attorney please feel free to do so." He gave her hand a final squeeze of dismissal. "Will you be able to get home?"

"I'll be fine," said Lucy. "Thanks for your concern."

He was already turning away from her, however, and draping an arm around Horowitz's shoulder.

"Now. Lieutenant," he was saying, "I want to assure you that the board will do everything it can to facilitate your investigation . . ."

Lucy went to retrieve her coat from Bitsy's office, where she had left it. She hesitated for a moment, then pushed open the door and stood in the doorway, struck with the way Bitsy's personality had filled the little room and trying to comprehend the fact that she would not be using it anymore. Her fingers would never pound the computer keyboard again, she would never reach for the pens and pencils stuffed in the English marmalade jar.

The office, of course, was just as she had left it. Little yellow stickies adorned the perimeter of the computer screen, the desk was covered with a sea of papers, and the windowsill was stacked with books and bound reports. Pictures and notes had spread far beyond the confines of the bulletin board, nearly covering one entire wall. Lucy paused and studied them.

There were postcards sent by authors and publishers announcing new books, nametags from conferences such as the New England Bookseller's Association's annual meeting in Boston, and clippings from book reviews. There were lots of notecards, too, mostly thank-you notes from grateful patrons who appreciated Bitsy's efforts to get them hard-to-find information and obscure books. There were even drawings made by the children who attended story hour, including one by Zoe.

Lucy reached out to unpin it.

"What do you think you're doing?" demanded an authoritative male voice.

Lucy jumped and turned to see a youthful state trooper holding a roll of yellow crime scene tape.

"My daughter made this drawing — I wanted it as a keepsake," she explained.

"I'm sorry — my orders are that nobody is to touch anything."

"I hardly think this qualifies as evidence," argued Lucy, withdrawing a push pin from the corner of Zoe's crayon portrait. "Besides, I'd be happy to sign a receipt or something."

"I'm sorry," he said. "I was just about to seal this room. You'll have to go. Please put the pin back just as it was."

"May I take my coat?" snapped Lucy, angry with the trooper's inflexible attitude.

He nodded and Lucy snatched it up, feeling like a criminal for attempting to take her own daughter's drawing. She glared at him as she left, then marched across the circulation area to the door, shrugging her arms into the sleeves as she went. She flung the doors open, hardly noticing the collection of official vans and police cars parked in front of the library, and ran down the stairs and along the path to the parking lot. She yanked the car door open and sat down hard in the driver's seat. She fumbled in her purse, looking for the ignition key and when she couldn't find it, burst into tears. She sat there, gripping the steering wheel and sobbing out loud, feeling both relieved and utterly ridiculous. When the tears finally stopped, she wiped her eyes and checked her coat pocket for the car keys. Finding them, she started the engine.

Driving more slowly than usual, she followed the familiar streets to Juanita's house. As she rolled down Elm Street she spotted a police cruiser parked in front of a large Victorian mansion that had seen better days. The original clapboard had been replaced with asbestos siding that was showing its age despite a coat of paint. A rickety metal fire escape was tacked to one side, indicating the house had been cut up into apartments. That must be where Bitsy lived, she thought, slowing the car.

She remembered Bitsy complaining

about her landlady, and dredged her memory for the woman's name. Willoughby? Wetherby? Withers! That was it! A honk from behind prompted the realization that the car had practically stopped, so Lucy pulled over to the side and gave the puzzled driver a wave. She sat there for a minute, observing the house and wondering if she dared pay a visit to Mrs. Withers.

There were some questions she'd like to ask her. Had Bitsy had any visitors lately? Had she seemed upset? Was she involved in a relationship?

Lucy was just about to get out of the car when she spotted a police officer coming around the side of the house. He climbed the steps to the front door and rang the bell, then stood waiting for the door to open. After his second ring the door did open and Lucy got a glimpse of Mrs. Withers, who was dressed in a bright orange sweater and garish brown and green plaid pants.

Disappointed at this lost opportunity, Lucy pulled out from the curb and drove on to the Orensteins' house. Juanita was obviously bursting with curiosity when she opened the door, but tactfully restrained herself from questioning Lucy about the morning's events.

"Are you all right, Lucy? You still look a little shaky. Can I give you a cup of tea or some lunch?" she asked, taking Lucy's arm and drawing her into the warm living room where Zoe and Sadie were playing with Barbie dolls. Rows of the leggy creatures were sitting on the sofa, and more were carefully arranged on bright pink plastic doll furniture set out on the carpeted floor.

"No, thanks. I'm really okay. I just want to get home." She sighed. "Zoe, it's time to go. Can you help clean up the toys, please?"

"Never mind," said Juanita. "Sadie can do it later. Come on, Zoe. Let's find your coat."

"Thanks for everything," said Lucy, when Zoe was suited up against the cold and ready to go.

"It was nothing," Juanita told her. "Sadie always enjoys having Zoe visit."

As they trudged through the snowy yard to the car, Lucy noticed that the bright sunlight of the morning was gone. The sky was filling up once again with heavy gray clouds. She sniffed the air.

"I smell snow," she told Zoe, helping her climb into her booster seat and snapping the seatbelt.

"You can't smell snow," said Zoe, laughing.

"Oh, yes, you can," said Lucy, once again starting the car.

As she drove, her mind kept going back to the moment when she found Bitsy's body. It was as if her thoughts were a broken video tape that kept replaying the same image over and over. She kept trying to get past it, just as she tended to fast-forward a rented movie through the violent parts, but her mind would not cooperate. It was stuck on Bitsy's murder.

Tears pricked at her eyes, and she tried to blink them back as she came to the steep climb up Red Top Road. She down-shifted for the climb, and the Subaru obligingly chugged up the hill toward home.

The house was empty. Lucy glanced at the clock and was shocked to see it was only two-thirty. She would have guessed it was much later.

"I'm hungry," said Zoe, pointedly eying the cookie jar.

"Good idea," said Lucy, remembering that she hadn't had any lunch. She put the kettle on to heat and set a plate of chocolate chip cookies on the kitchen table. Then she scooped some hot chocolate mix into two mugs and waited for the water to boil.

Damn Horowitz, she thought. What business did he have accusing her like that in front of all the others? Even if it was a little joke. And why was he joking anyway about something as terrible as murder? It was just a job for him — he didn't know or care about Bitsy. It didn't matter to him who the killer was so long as he caught him. Or her. The thought gave Lucy pause. Of course it could be a woman — a woman could shoot a gun just as effectively as a man.

She jumped as the kettle shrieked, and filled the mugs. Sitting down at the table opposite Zoe, she stirred her hot cocoa. Thank goodness the other kids were still at school — she wasn't ready to deal with the noise and confusion they brought home with them.

"Careful — it's hot," she warned Zoe.

"I know, Mom."

"Good."

Lucy lifted the mug to her lips. It felt heavy and she used two hands so it wouldn't spill. This is ridiculous, she thought, feeling that all her energy had somehow drained from her body. The little chores she ought to be doing seemed impossibly difficult. All she could do was sit.

This is depression, she decided. Shock and depression, compounded by low blood sugar. She made herself take a sip of cocoa, and then another.

If only she didn't feel so responsible. She knew it was absurd. She was the newest person on the board; she hadn't had time to do anything. But still she couldn't help feeling that she should have done something to prevent Bitsy's death. How could such a thing happen? And in the library, of all places?

They should have had a security system. But if one of the directors did kill Bitsy, as Horowitz seemed to think, it wouldn't have made any difference. Lucy put her head in her hands. How could she go back? How could she ever face those people, wondering all the time if one of them was a murderer?

Horowitz and his "mind your own business" be damned, she thought. There was only one way she could get through this, and it was by finding the murderer as soon as possible. She couldn't wait for the police to muddle their way through the case — that could take months, especially if the board members retained lawyers as she expected they would. The police wouldn't get very far unless they found some hard physical evidence, like the gun. She was the first one on the scene, however, and she hadn't seen anything.

That meant they would have to depend on questioning the suspects, but she didn't think these particular suspects were likely to submit themselves to that. They had nothing to gain and everything to lose; it was far safer to say nothing.

Of course, they would talk among themselves — that was human nature. They would have plenty to say to each other that they wouldn't want to share with the police. She drummed her fingers on the table. Tomorrow, she decided, she'd make a point of paying a visit to Miss Tilley. Horowitz could hardly call it meddling — after all, she would only be doing what any good neighbor would do. Paying a friendly visit to an elderly neighbor and having a nice little chat.

"Mom, can I have some more cocoa?" asked Zoe.

Lucy heard the roar of the school bus as it began the slow climb up the hill. Sara and Elizabeth and Toby would be home any minute.

"I guess I better heat up enough for the whole gang," she said, giving Zoe a little hug and tickling her tummy. "There's nothing like cocoa on a cold day."

The door flew open and Toby and Elizabeth jostled each other, each trying to be the first one in. Sara brought up the rear, her plump, round face red with anger.

"It's not fair! I never get to use the computer!" she screamed hoarsely at her older brother and sister.

Elizabeth and Toby weren't there to hear her. They had already vanished into the family room, shedding hats and scarves and coats as they went.

Lucy followed, and found them huddled over the computer, eyes fixed on the screen.

"Come on, come on," chanted Toby impatiently. "This thing takes forever to boot — I don't know why they didn't get a Pentium 90."

"Too cheap," commiserated Elizabeth. "I'm amazed they got anything at all."

"Don't you want some cocoa?" asked Lucy. "How was school?"

"Later, Mom. We're busy." Toby's eyes didn't waver from the screen as he clicked the mouse with his enormous hand. He was a junior in high school and already topped six feet; Lucy had trouble finding clothes and shoes big enough for him.

"Look at the mess you've made — aren't you going to hang up your coats and things?"

"Sure, Mom," said Elizabeth, brushing her short, dark hair out of her eyes, which were also fixed on the screen. "We'll do it later — we want to do this first."

Lucy was dismayed but right now she didn't have the energy to make them behave in a civilized manner. "Okay, just don't forget," she muttered, returning to the kitchen. It could be worse, she thought. They could be experimenting with drugs or sex or vandalizing some building. At least the Internet was supposed to be educational, even if it didn't do much for one's social graces.

"Mom, it's not fair," insisted Sara, who was pouring herself some cocoa. "I never get to use the computer. Elizabeth and Toby won't let me."

"We'll have to figure something out," said Lucy. "Why don't you take Zoe sliding when you finish your cocoa?"

"That's no fun," grumbled Sara, stuffing her chubby cheeks with cookies. "I want to play 'Zoroaster'."

"One cookie at a time, please, and don't forget to chew," reminded Lucy, reaching for the ringing phone.

"Hi, Ted," she said, recognizing his voice. Ted Stillings was the chief reporter, editor, and publisher of the local weekly newspaper, *The Pennysaver.* "I guess you must have heard."

"Gosh, Lucy, you might've given me a call," he complained.

Lucy occasionally worked at the paper, filling in for Ted's assistant, Phyllis, in addition to writing features on a freelance basis.

"I knew it was too late for this week — the paper came out today."

"Yeah, but I would've liked to get some on-the-scene coverage for next week."

"No chance of that, I'm afraid. The state police got right there."

"Well, you were there. What can you tell me?"

"Not much," said Lucy. "Like the other directors, I'm shocked and saddened by this dreadful event."

"Come on, Lucy," coaxed Ted. "You can't do this to me. You're a reporter, for God's sake."

"I'm a freelance feature writer," she corrected him. "And besides, I've already been warned by Horowitz to mind my own business."

"You know you're not going to let a little

thing like that stop you. Come on, tell me what you know."

"Well," drawled Lucy, yielding to Ted's coaxing, "Horowitz definitely thinks one of the directors is the murderer, but I just can't see it."

"Because they're all such upstanding citizens?"

"No — because they were more or less all together all morning. I don't think anybody had enough time. I think it must have been somebody from outside. Bitsy must have had a personal life away from the library. It could have been a jilted boyfriend, somebody like that. What have you heard?"

"I haven't talked to too many people yet. I did get some background stuff — I had her resumé in my files, from the selectmen's meeting when she was hired."

"Where'd she come from?"

"Massapequa, Long Island. She worked in a library there."

"Does she have family there? An ex-husband?"

"You know, I just don't know. I interviewed her for a profile piece when she first took the job. I pulled it out but it didn't really have much information. When I thought about it, I remembered being kind of frustrated because she wouldn't answer any personal questions. Just talked about all her plans for the library, how much she liked living in Maine, stuff like that."

"Maybe she had something to hide," suggested Lucy. "Maybe that's why she was killed."

"Could be," admitted Ted, "but so far I haven't found out much. I hope I can turn up something for next week's paper."

"At least you've got plenty of time."

"Yeah," said Ted. "So where's that story on gambling that you tell me you're working on? Can I expect it anytime soon?"

"Soon," hedged Lucy.

"Like when?" pressed Ted.

"Next Friday?"

"Can't you do it in time for next week's paper?"

"No way," said Lucy.

"Okay, but I'm counting on you, Lucy. Friday at the latest."

"I won't let you down," promised Lucy.

"Sure," said Ted, sounding skeptical.

As Lucy replaced the receiver she heard a commotion in the family room. Sara had evidently attempted to gain access to the computer, prompting outraged protests from Toby and Elizabeth.

"Enough!" she announced, marching over to the machine and turning the power switch off.

"You're not supposed to do that!" screamed Elizabeth. "You'll wreck it!"

"She's right, Mom," added Toby.

"I don't care," Lucy said through clenched teeth, placing her hands on her hips. "It's been a very long day and I want some peace and quiet. I want you to pick up your coats and hats off the floor and then go outside and have some good old-fashioned fun in the snow. Do you understand me?"

"Do we have to?" groaned Toby, looking at her as if she were completely mad.

"Yes, you do," insisted Lucy. "And have a good time, too!"

The kids clattered out obediently; Lucy suspected they'd be sneaking back into the warm house before long. She had better enjoy the peace and quiet while she could. She piled a few pillows at one end of the couch and lay down, closing her eyes and trying to empty her mind of all thoughts.

After a few minutes, she realized it was futile. Her mind was buzzing with questions. Why had Bitsy left Massapequa? Why did she choose Maine, of all places?

Did she have a special reason for coming to Tinker's Cove? And if she hadn't come to Tinker's Cove, would she have been murdered? Why did she die?

Before she realized what she had done, Lucy was back on her feet and heading for the kitchen. It was too late today; she had to get supper started. But tomorrow, she decided, she was going to start looking for some answers.

Six

*Little Red Riding Hood decided to pay
a visit to her grandmother.*

On Friday morning Lucy looked out the window and saw a snow squall. The wind was tossing some fine little flakes around, but there wasn't enough snow for school to be closed. Lucy sent up a little prayer of thanksgiving when the school bus carried the three older kids off in the morning, then she started tidying up the kitchen. She was just wiping off the counter when Bill came in looking for his lunchbox before leaving for work. A skilled restoration carpenter, he had been hired by a nearby church to reconstruct a wineglass pulpit that had begun to wobble dangerously, putting the minister on decidedly shaky footing when he gave his sermon.

"What's on the menu today?" he asked, opening the lunchbox and taking a peek.

"A meatloaf sandwich and a thermos of vegetable soup." Lucy always tried to include something hot. She knew that the congregation's budget didn't provide for heating the sanctuary on weekdays and Bill's space heater couldn't begin to warm the entire church.

"Mmmm," said Bill, snapping it shut and setting it on the kitchen table so he could zip his jacket. He looked at her thoughtfully. "Lucy, are you all right about this Bitsy thing?"

"As all right as I can be, I guess," said Lucy. "It isn't as if we were close friends."

"That's right," said Bill. "She must have been hanging around with some pretty desperate characters to get herself killed. It's no business of yours, and I hope you'll leave it to the police."

Lucy started to protest but he grabbed her hand and pulled her to him, folding her in his arms.

"I couldn't stand it if anything happened to you."

Lucy looked into his eyes and stroked his beard, now tinged with gray. "Don't worry," she said, placing her hands on his chest and gently pushing him away. "Horowitz has already warned me to mind my own business."

"Sounds like good advice," said Bill, putting on his gloves. "I hope you'll take it."

"I intend to. Besides, I don't have time to investigate — Ted's after me to finish a story for him," said Lucy, reaching up to pull Bill's watch cap down over his ears. "It's cold out there — stay warm, okay?"

"Okay." He gave her a quick kiss and was gone.

A glance at the kitchen clock told Lucy it was a few minutes past eight. If she was lucky, she thought, she might just catch Horowitz at his office.

Before she had time to think better of it, she punched in the number of his direct line. As she listened to the rings she chewed her lip nervously.

"Horowitz."

"Umm, Lieutenant, uhh, this is Lucy Stone," she stammered.

"Ah. Good morning, Mrs. Stone."

"You can call me Lucy," she invited, wondering what his first name might be.

"That's all right, Mrs. Stone. Is there a reason for this call?"

"Actually, there is. There's something I forgot to tell you yesterday."

"And what's that?"

"Well, when I went to find Bitsy, a whole box of art supplies was spilled on the stairs. It looked as if she was going to have

85

the kids make valentines — there were lace doilies and red construction paper and scissors and crayons all over." She paused. "Do you think it's important? Maybe she encountered the killer on the stairs?"

"Or maybe she just tripped," said Horowitz.

"In that case, wouldn't she have picked up the mess?"

"I doubt it," sighed Horowitz. "From what I've seen of her, she never cleaned anything up that could be left for later."

"Have you searched her apartment?" probed Lucy, determined to take advantage of Horowitz's unexpectedly chatty mood.

"We're working on it," he admitted, before catching himself. "Mrs. Stone, didn't I tell you to leave this investigation to the police?"

"I just thought you ought to know about the spilled art supplies," said Lucy, sounding hurt. "I was trying to be helpful."

"Well, thanks."

The line was dead; Horowitz had hung up.

Lucy replaced the receiver and finished tidying the kitchen, then pried Zoe away from "Bunny Beware" and got her dressed for Kiddie Kollege. As a four-year-old she attended three mornings a week, on Mondays, Wednesdays, and Fridays.

After leaving Zoe in her basement classroom at the town's recreation center, Lucy stopped in at the day care center just down the hall where her friend, Sue Finch, worked.

When she entered, Sue was helping a little boy out of his winter jacket. She looked up and gave Lucy a big smile.

"I was hoping you'd stop by," she said, tucking her glossy pageboy behind her ears.

"I guess you heard," said Lucy. "That's a cute sweater," she added, noticing the embroidered design that showed Mary coming to school with her little lamb.

"It's not really my style," said Sue, who preferred tailored, sophisticated clothing. "But the kids love this kind of stuff." She propped her hand on her hip and cocked her head. "So, tell me all about it. Did you really discover Bitsy's body?"

"Don't remind me," groaned Lucy.

"Was it awful?" asked Sue, stepping closer and whispering so the children wouldn't hear.

"What do you think? She was shot!"

Sue patted her shoulder. "Poor thing. It

must have been quite a shock." She thought for a minute. "How did the kids take it?"

"Zoe was with me — but she didn't see anything. Actually, she didn't seem bothered at all. In fact, she said Bitsy was mean and story hour wasn't much fun anyway."

"Kids can be so . . ." Sue looked for a word to finish the sentence.

"Honest?" suggested Lucy.

"That wasn't exactly the word I was looking for, but it will do. Poor Bitsy didn't have a clue about kids." Sue surveyed the bright and homey day care center, where a dozen little ones were happily occupied.

"I always liked her," said Lucy. "She was a breath of fresh air after Miss Tilley. She started bringing in new books — the kind people like to read. Bestsellers and popular authors. And she was friendly. Didn't make you feel like a thief for borrowing a book." She fiddled with the zipper tag on her jacket. "I can't imagine why anyone would want to kill her."

"She must have had a life outside the library," said Sue. "I'll bet it was a boyfriend or something." She narrowed her eyes mischievously. "Isn't it usually the boyfriend? You're the expert, after all."

"I'm no expert — and I don't think Bitsy had a boyfriend."

"Well," said Sue slowly, turning her attention to two little boys at the sand table. "Sand isn't for throwing, Peter. Why don't you see how many shovels it takes to fill the truck?" She turned back to Lucy. "You know, she might have gone just a bit too far with the wrong person."

"What do you mean?" Lucy was mystified.

"You know — all the personal comments she made. Like when I took out a book about gardening. It was August and Sidra had just gone back to college. Bitsy concluded I was suffering from empty nest syndrome. 'Looking for a new hobby now that your baby has left home?' she asked. 'No,' I told her. 'My daylilies are looking kind of straggly.' "

"They need to be divided."

"I know that now," said Sue, keeping an eye on the sand table. "That's exactly what the book said. And I followed the directions and I expect I'll have outstanding daylilies this summer." She looked out the window at the lightly falling snow and added, "If summer ever comes."

"I don't see how something like that could get her killed," said Lucy. "She just liked to make conversation."

"Peter — I'm warning you. If you keep throwing sand at Justin you'll have to go to time-out." Sue turned back to Lucy and nodded knowingly. "Everybody's got secrets, and this is a very small town. It wouldn't be hard to hit a nerve — somebody looking up bankruptcy information or stuff about divorce . . ."

"A book about poisons, maybe?" asked Lucy, but Sue didn't answer. She was headed for the sand table.

"I'll call you later, Lucy," she said, raising her hand in a wave.

Lucy thought about what Sue had said as she headed over to the Quik-Stop. Maybe she had a point. Bitsy loved to make conversation but her friendly questions could be misinterpreted, especially by somebody who had something to hide. Pulling into the parking lot at the combination gas station and convenience store, she wondered if Bitsy had been less popular than she had thought. She braked and climbed out of the car, noticing a fresh scattering of discarded lottery tickets mixed in with the falling snow that was blowing about. She wondered how many more worthless tickets were buried in the accumulated snow that covered the ground.

A bell on the door tinkled when she went inside and a pretty girl at the cash register looked up.

"What can I do for you today?" she asked politely.

"I'm not here to buy anything," Lucy apologized. "I write for *The Pennysaver* and I'm working on a story about gambling, especially the state lottery. Can you answer some questions for me?"

"Sure." The girl gave a little shrug.

"First, I need your name," said Lucy, getting her notebook out of her shoulder bag and uncapping her pen.

"Lois Kirwan."

"Oh, I know Dot," said Lucy. In fact, everybody knew Dot, who worked as a cashier at Marzetti's IGA. "Is she your mother?"

"Mother-in-law," said the girl. "I'm married to Tommy."

"That's nice," said Lucy, getting down to business. "Well, what I wondered is how big a business are these lottery tickets? Do you sell a lot of them?"

Lois nodded. "We must sell hundreds, even thousands."

"Is that in a week?"

"No." Lois chuckled. "That's in a day."

"I had no idea," said Lucy.

"I've seen people spend their entire paychecks on scratch tickets." She paused and leaned across the counter. "I'm not supposed to — the owner would have a fit if he knew — but I tell them it's a waste of money. You can't beat the system. These tickets come in rolls of five hundred and sell for a dollar apiece. On average, the winning tickets total three hundred dollars. It's a losing proposition. It has to be or the state wouldn't make any money."

"How much of the store's business is lottery tickets?" asked Lucy.

"Most of it — I'd guess at least half. Then there's cigarettes — that's probably the other half."

"What about milk and bread?" That was all that Lucy ever bought at the Quik-Stop herself.

"Hardly anybody buys anything here without buying at least one lottery ticket, too. Lots of times, if they have a five or a ten dollar bill, they'll take the change in scratch tickets."

Lucy was shocked at this extravagance. "Is there a typical buyer?" she asked.

"Everybody buys them. Except kids — we can't sell them if you're under eighteen."

"What about the people who buy a lot at one time?"

"They tend to be older — and mostly men. There's one man — he's really distinguished looking. Like he's rich. Nice overcoat. Beautiful leather gloves. Drives a big Lincoln. He comes in at least once a week and buys a lot of tickets. Fifty minimum, sometimes a lot more. At least he can afford it. A lot of them, well, you know they're emptying out their wallets and poking around under the car seats to scrape together enough change to buy a ticket. It's sad. It's such a waste of money."

"They're hoping they'll get lucky and strike it rich," said Lucy. "Have you had any big winners who bought tickets here?"

"I've never had a big winner on a scratch ticket but we've had some pretty big Lotto winners." She pointed to a picture frame on the wall behind her that contained three Lotto stubs. "I think one was a hundred thousand dollars. We never had a million dollar winner. George — he's the owner — keeps telling me we're due." She shook her head in disapproval. "He tells the customers that, too. He thinks the lottery is the greatest. He's always putting up the signs the lottery commission sends." She paused and rolled her eyes, indicating the large number of colorful advertisements stuck up all over the store. "Like we don't have enough already. And if the Lotto pot is bigger than usual he wants me to mention it to all the customers."

"Do you ever play?" asked Lucy.

"Me? No way. I've got a jar at home I put all my spare change in. Last year I had enough to buy a new sofa."

"You're a smart girl."

"Yeah, too smart to stay in this job. I've got my name in at the bank. As soon as there's an opening, I'm outta here." The bell jangled and she turned to help a customer.

"Thanks for all your help," said Lucy, concluding the interview so Lois could get back to work. "Good luck with the bank job."

"Hey," said Lois, turning to tear off a handful of scratch tickets. "You make your own luck, know what I mean?"

Lucy gave her notebook a satisfied little pat as she left the store. Thanks to Lois she had gotten some good quotes she could use in her story. She'd love to talk to the owner, George, to find out exactly how much of his business came from the lottery but doubted he'd cooperate. In her experience, small-business owners tended to be close-mouthed when it came to facts and figures.

She climbed in the car and started the engine. If only she knew someone who was a compulsive gambler, she thought, or a recovered compulsive gambler. That would give the story a face, someone the readers could identify with.

At least she had a good start, she thought, backing the car around and turning onto Main Street. The next step was to get some information from the lottery commission. But before she tackled that, she wanted to pay a little visit to Miss Tilley.

It was the least she could decently do, she rationalized. After all, she had been friends with the former librarian ever since she and Bill first moved to Tinker's Cove nearly twenty years ago. Furthermore, both she and Miss Tilley were members of the library board of directors. Paying a visit to a fragile and elderly colleague who was undoubtedly distressed by this violent turn of events could hardly be construed as attempting to investigate Bitsy's murder.

"I suppose you're investigating Bitsy's murder," said Miss Tilley, when Rachel Goodman admitted Lucy to the little antique Cape Cod house. Rachel worked mornings for Miss Tilley, taking care of the housekeeping and laundry and preparing a substantial midday meal for her.

"Can you stay for lunch?" asked Rachel. "I'm making fish chowder." Rachel's son Richie was good friends with Toby, and she and Lucy were well acquainted.

"It smells delicious," said Lucy, inhaling the rich fragrance. She guessed that Rachel would welcome some relief from Miss Tilley. "But I can only stay for an hour or so. I have to pick up Zoe at twelve."

"How about some tea, then?" offered Rachel, taking Lucy's coat.

"I'd love it. Thanks."

"Sit right down," invited Miss Tilley, who was ensconced in her favorite wing chair by the fireplace. She made a cozy picture, sitting beside the glowing fire with a colorful crocheted afghan warming her legs. "It's about time you got here. You have to get to the bottom of this."

"I've been told not to meddle," Lucy informed her dutifully. "Lieutenant Horowitz doesn't want me interfering in his investigation."

"Nonsense. You're in a far better position to discover who killed Bitsy than anyone else."

"I don't know about that," demurred Lucy, taking the tea from Rachel.

"I have work to do in the kitchen, so I'll leave you two to visit," said Rachel. A cloud seemed to pass over her usually sunny face. "It's just awful about Bitsy. I can hardly believe it really happened." She dabbed at her nose with a tissue and returned to the kitchen.

"I can believe it," said Miss Tilley. "I would have liked to strangle her a few times myself."

"Well, thinking about it and actually doing it are two separate things. There are times when we'd all like to do away with someone . . ."

"Bitsy asked for it," said Miss Tilley, smoothing the afghan with gnarled fingers. "Right from day one."

"I'm really surprised to hear you say that," said Lucy. "I always thought she did a great job."

Miss Tilley threw up her hands in disgust. "Hardly. She was so disorganized. It was a scandal. Things were always such a mess."

"Her style was different from yours, but you have to admit that she did some good things." Lucy wanted to say that Bitsy was friendly and welcoming, but was afraid

Miss Tilley would be insulted. "A lot of people liked the way she ran things — more people than ever were using the library."

"Oh, she was Miss Nicey-nice to the patrons, I'll give you that. Never bothered with overdue fines, never even made the children wash their hands before they handled the books."

Lucy couldn't help smiling. She knew a lot of Tinker's Cove natives remembered Miss Tilley's insistence that they wash their "little finger bones" as soon as they entered the library.

"I know people think it was silly, but the library has always had a limited budget," continued Miss Tilley. "Making the children wash their hands saved quite a bit of wear and tear on expensive books. But that's neither here nor there." She waved her blue-veined hand back and forth. "The point I was trying to make is that she talked about people behind their backs."

"You're not the first person I've heard say that."

"Oh, yes," nodded Miss Tilley. "For instance, if you took out a book on, oh, say sexual dysfunction, Bitsy would notice. And she'd talk about it. She'd mention it to the next person who came along, and the next. And each time she'd embellish it. First it would be 'Guess who took out a book on sexual dysfunction.' Then it would be 'I guess Lucy Stone is having some problems with Bill'. Before the day was out she'd have you considering divorce because you and Bill were sexually incompatible!"

"Did she really say those things about me?" said Lucy, feeling rather sick.

"Oh, I don't know. I was just using you as an example." She took a sip of tea and looked at Lucy over her teacup. "But I don't see why not you, too. She talked about everybody."

"After Zoe was born I took out a book on abnormal psychology and she asked me if I was suffering from post-partum depression," recalled Lucy.

"I heard about that," volunteered Rachel, returning with the teapot.

"I never had post-partum depression!" exclaimed Lucy.

"Everybody thought you did," said Rachel. "I was so relieved when I saw you'd gotten over it."

"I never had it," insisted Lucy.

"Okay. I believe you," Rachel said diplomatically. "More tea?"

"No, thanks," said Lucy, furrowing her

brow thoughtfully. "I don't know — this seems kind of a stretch. What kind of secret could she have found out that would be damaging enough that somebody would have to kill her? Besides, she's done a lot of good. Just look at the new addition — that would never have happened without Bitsy."

"That's the most ridiculous thing I've ever heard, Lucy Stone!" Miss Tilley was quivering with rage. "That is absolutely untrue! I don't know where you got an idea like that! The board decided to build the addition, and the board raised the money. Bitsy had nothing to do with it!"

"I'm sorry," said Lucy, hastening to make amends. "I must have misunderstood."

"You certainly did. In fact, all Bitsy contributed to the fund-raising effort were some harebrained ideas. She proposed using the endowment fund, said it was too little money to bother about keeping, and she even suggested we sell Josiah's Tankard to buy computers. As if computers will ever replace books! But she wouldn't hear it — all she ever talked about was computer-this and computer-that! I don't know what people see in those newfangled machines anyway."

Lucy thought of her struggle to disengage Zoe from the computer earlier that morning and smiled. "They're certainly not all they're cracked up to be. Sometimes they're more trouble than they're worth."

"My thoughts exactly," said Miss Tilley. "And most of the board members agreed with me."

"So Bitsy was out of favor with the board?"

"She certainly was. In fact, I had suggested taking steps toward dismissing her. It's tricky these days, you know. People sue for wrongful dismissal. Chuck told us we had to be very careful and begin documenting all the reasons why we were unhappy with her." She paused and smacked her lips. "Now we won't have to bother with all that. Looks like whoever killed that creature did the board a big favor."

"That's a terrible thing to say." Lucy was truly shocked. "Maybe you didn't like her, but she didn't deserve to die!" She paused a moment. "And she wasn't a 'creature' — she was a person."

"I have a right to my opinion," the old woman said stubbornly. "And I can call her a creature if I want to."

"Well, not to me, you can't," said Lucy.

She was appalled at her old friend's attitude. She got to her feet and placed her cup and saucer on Miss Tilley's antique tavern table, then looked straight at the old woman. "You're really going too far. I'm not going to listen to talk like this."

Rachel, who had overheard them in the kitchen, hurried out and got Lucy's coat out of the closet. She held it up and whispered in Lucy's ear as she slipped her arms into the sleeves.

"Don't pay any mind when she says things like that — she's just getting old and she doesn't like it."

Lucy squeezed Rachel's hand. "You're a saint to put up with an old witch like her," she said, not bothering to lower her voice. "Thanks for the tea."

From the doorway, Rachel called after her, "Take it easy, Lucy."

As she walked to the car, Lucy heard Miss Tilley's quavering voice.

"I don't know what she's got so high and mighty about!" she declared as Rachel closed the door.

Seven

Three little kittens,
They lost their mittens,
And they began to cry . . .

The snow squalls had stopped when Lucy left Miss Tilley's, and the sun was making a half-hearted attempt to break through the clouds. It didn't look as if it had much of a chance, Lucy thought glumly; the slim opening between the clouds was getting narrower by the minute. She shivered and pulled her hat down over her ears and got in the car.

She turned the key in the ignition and pushed the heater controls up to maximum. Then she pulled away from the curb, neglecting to check for traffic. The loud honk of a horn as a pick-up truck swerved to avoid the Subaru made her jump.

Why am I so upset, she asked herself as she carefully checked her mirrors. Driving slowly along the snow-packed road, she wondered why she had found Miss Tilley's attitude so disturbing. She hadn't been especially good friends with Bitsy, after all, and Bitsy certainly hadn't minded spreading rumors about her. Still, she couldn't help but be saddened by her death. It was horrible and shocking, but, she realized, dwelling on it wasn't getting her anywhere. She had a few minutes before she had to pick up Zoe, so she decided to stop at the IGA.

The automatic door opened for her and she took a shopping cart. The fluorescent lights made the aging store look dreary; it was nothing like the shiny new superstore that had opened out on the Interstate. Nevertheless, it offered a change from the gray monotony of winter in Maine.

Lucy stopped at the magazine rack and leafed through one of the women's magazines but decided she didn't want to get organized and wasn't interested in perking up her wardrobe or spicing up favorite family meals. What she really wanted to know was who killed Bitsy, and why, information she wasn't going to find in *Family Circle*. She replaced the magazine and slowly pushed the cart along, pausing at the meagre display of fresh flowers and potted plants.

Why didn't they ever have anything but those ghastly carnations? The red color was an unpleasant reminder of Bitsy's blood, spreading out on the gray industrial tile of the workroom. She picked up a little polka-dot plant in a pink pot and examined it; it didn't look worth three ninety-nine so she put it back.

Dispirited, she pushed on to the produce department, wishing that she hadn't gotten so angry at Miss Tilley. She shouldn't have reacted the way she did; half of what Miss Tilley said was for effect. She loved to shock people, and she had certainly succeeded this morning. Lucy had found the old woman's callousness toward Bitsy's death shocking, but sometimes it seemed to her that old people didn't react in quite the same way to death as younger people. She remembered her own grandfather checking the obituaries every morning and his satisfaction when he occasionally discovered he'd outlived a younger acquaintance.

"Never touched a drop and wouldn't eat red meat," he'd comment. "Didn't do him much good, did it?"

She smiled to herself, remembering a spry old fellow in a plaid flannel shirt neatly topped with a bow tie, and khaki pants held up by suspenders. He certainly enjoyed an occasional glass of whiskey, and insisted on meat and potatoes for dinner every night. Grandma's occasional experiments with spaghetti and Spanish rice had not been successful. He had lived to be eighty-five even though he never ate a raw vegetable and considered fruit unfit for human consumption unless it was baked inside a pie crust.

Lucy reached for a bag of oranges and, on further consideration, added a bag of grapefruit. Even if the board members had favored Bitsy, she thought, they would have been thoroughly dismayed by her proposal to sell Josiah's Tankard. An idea like that would have lost her some friends, that was for sure.

She stopped, resting her forearms on the handle of the cart, and considered a display of cereal. Now that she'd had time to think it over, Miss Tilley's attitude toward Bitsy wasn't really all that surprising. Miss Tilley had devoted her life to the library; she had worked there for fifty years or more. It was much more than a job to her. The library contained everything she held dearest in life, including Josiah's Tankard. She must have been deeply hurt when she was forced to retire and her job was given to Bitsy. And it certainly didn't help matters that Bitsy's attitudes were so radically different from hers.

If Miss Tilley was entitled to dislike Bitsy, if she regarded her as an enemy, Lucy guessed she couldn't blame her for taking some satisfaction in her demise. Putting it that way made it seem better, she decided. "Demise" was a much nicer word than "murder".

Miss Tilley was just reacting in a very human way. Queen Elizabeth I probably indulged in a chuckle or two when she succeeded in detaching Mary, Queen of Scots' head from her neck.

And besides, she was never going to get to the bottom of this without Miss Tilley's help, she decided. Miss Tilley knew everything about everybody in town, and who had what skeletons hidden in which closet. She also knew a lot about Bitsy, even though that knowledge was tainted with disapproval. There was no way around it, Lucy concluded, pushing the cart to the check-out: she was going to have to apologize to Miss Tilley.

As she stood in line, Lucy regarded the woman in front of her. She was wearing a bright pink parka that certainly didn't complement her green-and-brown plaid polyester pants.

"Mrs. Withers!" exclaimed Lucy.

"Yes?" The woman turned, revealing a round face with narrow lips, brightly outlined in fuchsia lipstick.

"You don't know me," began Lucy. "I'm Lucy Stone. I was the one who found Bitsy Howell yesterday."

"The police said she was shot." Mrs. Withers looked doubtful. "That so?"

"Oh, yes." Lucy nodded. "Do you have any idea who might have done it? Did she have a fight with her boyfriend or anything like that?"

"Not likely. She didn't have no boyfriend. No friends at all, far as I could tell. Kept herself to herself." Mrs. Withers began unloading her cart onto the checkout conveyer.

"That was a terrible thing," added Dot, the cashier.

"It's really quite a loss for me," confessed Mrs. Withers sadly.

"You were close?" inquired Lucy.

"She was my tenant." Mrs. Withers's penciled eyebrows shot up. "The police have sealed the apartment! I don't know when I'm going to be able to move out her stuff and get it rented again."

"That's just normal procedure," said Dot, ringing up a box of cookies.

"What will happen to her things?" asked Lucy.

"I spoke to her family, in New York someplace. I asked when they were coming and what to do with it all, and you know what they said? They said just give it all to the Salvation Army!"

"Everything?" Lucy was shocked.

"Everything! Imagine that." Mrs. Withers's numerous chins quivered in indignation.

"Don't they want anything of hers? Something to remember her by?" asked Dot. "That'll be eight dollars and sixteen cents."

"Not a thing — said I should just get rid of it all," said Mrs. Withers, pulling her wallet out of her imitation leather purse. "Doesn't seem like they've got much family feeling, if you ask me."

"Poor Bitsy," sighed Lucy, reaching into her basket for the bag of oranges.

Back in the Subaru, driving down Main Street on her way to Kiddie Kollege, Lucy passed Hayden's antique shop, Northcross and Love. In the window she noticed a tavern table, similar to Miss Tilley's, with a couple of pewter tankards displayed on it. That was an idea, she thought. Miss Tilley might enjoy having a tankard similar to Josiah's Tankard. Of course, she couldn't afford one as old and valuable as Josiah's Tankard but she might find something that was less expensive. Even a reproduction. She resolved to come back to the shop when she had more time.

When she and Zoe got home, Lucy cut up some of the oranges and grapefruit and sprinkled a little dried coconut on top.

"It's called 'ambrosia'," she told Zoe.

Starved for vitamin C and sunshine, the two of them finished the entire bowl. Then Zoe scampered off to the family room, and Lucy got out her gambling notes. She put in a call to the state lottery commission for information and learned most of what she wanted was on the commission's website. Then she made a second call and left a message with Gamblers Anonymous. After that she called Ted to discuss the illustration for the story.

"We need some good art," she told him. "I was thinking of a photograph of discarded lottery tickets in a parking lot or something."

"I'll see what I can come up with," he

said. "Any luck getting some quotes from a problem gambler?"

"I've got a call in to Gamblers Anonymous, and I'm waiting for some info from the lottery commission. It's coming along. It would be a lot easier if I knew a compulsive gambler." She paused and studied the dirty lunch dishes that were still on the kitchen table. "What have you heard about the murder?"

"Not much. They're keeping a particularly tight lid on this one."

"Anything about the funeral arrangements?"

"Her family's made arrangements to have her cremated. There'll be a memorial service at a later date."

"That's about what I expected."

"Is the library board going to do anything?"

"I don't think so," said Lucy. "What I hear is that the board members weren't happy with Bitsy and at least some of them wanted to fire her."

"Bitsy?" Ted was astonished.

"I was surprised, too. I thought everybody loved her." Lucy heard the school bus, down at the bottom of the hill. "I've got to go — the kids are home. But you know, I heard something funny today, and it might be a motive for whoever killed her. It seems that Bitsy liked to gossip about the books people took out of the library. You know, like if you took out a book about alcoholism she would start telling other people."

"So what?"

"Well, from what I heard, she would start with the fact that you borrowed the book but pretty soon you would be a full-fledged alcoholic."

"Oh," said Ted, grasping the possibilities. "That would be a very dangerous thing to do in a town like this."

"I know," agreed Lucy as the kitchen door flew open and the kids blew in. " 'Bye."

She hung up the receiver and faced her offspring, a no-nonsense expression on her face.

"Boots on the newspaper under the radiator, please. Coats on hooks. Bookbags, well, anywhere except the kitchen floor. Got it?"

"Aye, aye!" said Toby, giving her a mock salute.

"Unnnh!" grunted Sara, tugging at her boots without bothering to untie them.

"You'd think we were idiots," grumbled Elizabeth. "It isn't as if we didn't know to hang up our coats."

Lucy decided to let that one go and started putting the lunch dishes in the dishwasher. The kitchen gradually emptied as the older kids finished taking off their snow gear, and Zoe appeared in the doorway.

"Toby made me stop playing computer," she complained.

"Well, you've been playing for hours. It's time to give somebody else a turn. Why not help me make some fruity Jell-O for dessert?"

After they had finished filling a mold with lemon-flavored gelatine studded with orange pieces, Lucy decided to see if one of the kids would help her access the lottery commission on the computer.

When she went into the family room, she found Toby, Elizabeth, and Sara huddled together over the keyboard. For once, they weren't fighting — whatever they were looking at was equally fascinating to all three. Lucy stood behind them and peered over their shoulders, but all she saw was line after line of text.

"Type in: I'm 18, I have long blond hair, and I have a 36-inch bust," prompted Elizabeth.

"Better make it 39 inches," said Toby,

prompting peals of giggles from the girls.

Wow! appeared on the screen. *I'd reelly like to meet you.*

"Stop it!" exclaimed Lucy. "He's probably some pervert."

"Mom, he's just some hopeless computer nerd in Chicago or somewhere," said Elizabeth with a toss of her short, black bangs.

"It's fun to get him going."

"He thinks we're a gorgeous blonde," said Sara, giggling.

"Well what if he finds out our address or something? He might even come here — what about that?"

"The only address he knows us by is B.Boobs." Toby was laughing.

"Are you sure?" Lucy was suspicious. "He doesn't know where we live?"

"No, Mom. This is cyberspace. For all he knows, B.Boobs lives in Norway." Toby clicked away at the keyboard. "That's a good idea — I'm going to put in something about fjords."

Lucy watched as the reply appeared on the screen: *Do girls in Norway wear bras?*

No, typed Toby, sending the girls into gales of laughter.

"Stop it! Right now! I can't believe your father and I spent thousands of dollars on a computer just so you can talk dirty with some weirdo," complained Lucy. "Anyway, I want you to find a website for me."

"Sure, Mom. What do you want?"

"I've got it here." Lucy consulted a slip of paper. "Three 'w's, a period, then 'm-e-l-o-t-t-o', another period and 'c-o-m'."

Toby clicked the mouse a few times and typed in the letters. "Here it is."

"Just like that?" Lucy was impressed.

"Sure. Here, take the mouse. You can click around and find what you want, okay?"

"What if I make a mistake?"

"You can't," shrugged Toby. "Just keep clicking. I'm going to get something to eat."

Lucy took his seat. Hesitantly, she tried moving the mouse. A little arrow zoomed across the screen. She pointed it at "About the Maine Lottery Commission" and clicked. Nothing happened.

"It's not working."

"Put the arrow on the letters," advised Sara.

Lucy adjusted it and clicked. A picture of lottery headquarters appeared.

"Look at that!" Lucy was impressed again, and waited for more. Nothing happened. "Is this all I get? Just a picture?"

"See the little arrow in the corner? Put the mouse there and hold it down."

Lucy followed Sara's instructions and text appeared, explaining the lottery's creation by a vote of the state legislature. Soon she was pulling up tables of sales by towns, average return to vendors, prize awards by town and county. She grabbed a pencil and started noting the information down on a piece of paper she extracted from the printer.

Toby returned and stood beside her, chewing on a sandwich. Lucy smelled peanut butter.

"You don't have to do that," he said. "You can print it out."

"I can?"

"Sure." Toby clicked the mouse a few times and the printer began humming and spewing out sheets of paper.

"Wow," Lucy said, awestruck. "I didn't know it could do this. This is amazing."

Toby patted her shoulder sympathetically. "You'll be okay, Mom. It's just 'future shock'."

Future shock . . . that was a good term for it, thought Lucy. Pleased as she was with the results of her Internet research, thanks to the kids she'd discovered that there was a definite downside to computers. Thinking of the various board members, she didn't think they would be as enthusiastic about putting the library on-line as Bitsy was. While she thought the kids' explorations of the Internet were harmless enough, even if they were a waste of time, she didn't think Ed or Gerald or Miss Tilley would agree. They certainly wouldn't want the town's youth to have access to the uncensored information available on the web.

But, she thought as she collected the sheets of paper from the printer, computers weren't the sort of issue that led to murder. Or were they?

Tomorrow, she decided, she'd pay a visit to Hayden's shop and see about those tankards. And since she was going to be there anyway, she might as well ask Hayden about Bitsy's relations with the board members.

Eight

Jack Sprat could eat no fat,
His wife could eat no lean,
Together
They licked the platter clean.

It was almost three o'clock on Saturday afternoon before Lucy got away for an hour or two of antiquing. But when she pulled open the heavy pine door, she discovered that Northcross and Love was not the type of antiques shop she was used to. There was no clutter of dusty, mismatched objects covering every available surface, no display cases crammed with bits and pieces of china and glassware and jewelry. Instead, a few highly polished pieces of furniture, carefully spotlighted, were arranged to suggest a homelike setting. A Queen Anne dining table stood on a tastefully faded Oriental rug with a Canton soup tureen serving as a centerpiece. Above it, a gleaming brass chandelier held at least a dozen hand-dipped

118

candles. It had not been converted to electricity; that would undoubtedly be considered heresy by the shop's clientele, who apparently took their antiques very seriously indeed.

Lucy turned the tag on one of the chairs arranged around the table and gasped when she saw the price was fifteen thousand dollars.

"Can I help you?"

Lucy looked up and saw Hayden standing in a doorway that led to the back of the store.

"Lucy — I didn't recognize you! This is a nice surprise." He was smiling warmly and seemed genuinely glad to see her. "I didn't know you were interested in antiques."

"I am, but I'm afraid you're a little bit beyond my price range," she said.

"We cater to serious collectors," said Hayden. "In fact, most of our business is through the computer and our customers are scattered all over the country."

"I had no idea," said Lucy. "I do most of my buying at flea markets and auctions."

"You can still find nice things, but it's getting harder. Are you interested in anything in particular?" He cocked his head, and looked at her over his half-glasses. In a

Harris tweed sport coat, bow tie, and tasseled loafers, Hayden was the very picture of a country gentleman.

"Yesterday I saw two pewter tankards in the window, but I notice that they're gone."

Hayden was crestfallen. "I just packed them up — they're going to California. If I'd known you were interested I would have let you know."

"I probably couldn't have afforded them, anyway. Do you mind telling me . . . ?"

"Not at all." He smiled sympathetically. "The pair went for twenty."

"Twenty dollars?" Lucy's hopes revived.

"Twenty thousand."

"Oh."

"You're new to pewter?" inquired Hayden.

"Very new — I don't know much about it at all. It's not for me. I'm looking for a gift. For Miss Tilley, in fact. I thought she might like having something like Josiah's Tankard."

"That's a lovely idea." Hayden nodded in approval, and his bald head shone in the intense light from the overhead spots. "Is it her birthday? I should send a card."

"No." Lucy couldn't resist the urge to confess to this pleasant man. "I had a disagreement with her, about Bitsy. I want to give her the tankard as an apology."

"Miss T. never approved of Bitsy." He clucked his tongue. "It was classic, really. She ran the library for more than thirty years. She didn't want to retire — the board really had to force her out. It was very difficult." He gave a little shudder. "It was obvious that the job was getting to be too much for her, but she simply would not admit it."

"I know. I remember when she had that awful accident and nearly killed Jennifer Mitchell. She kept insisting it wasn't her fault — she wanted to keep on driving!"

Hayden shook his head, amazed at this example of the foolishness of the older generation. "Lucy, my partner and I usually have a coffee break around now — will you join us?"

"Sure," agreed Lucy with a big smile. "I never say no to coffee."

He led her to a surprisingly modern and efficient office area in the rear of the store where a tall, lean man in a plaid shirt and jeans was pounding on the buttons of a fax machine.

"Ralph, stop abusing that machine," said Hayden. "There's someone I want you to meet."

Ralph turned, revealing a ruggedly handsome face that reminded Lucy of Gregory Peck in his early movies.

"Ralph, this is Lucy Stone. She's a fellow sufferer on the library board."

"I'm pleased to make your acquaintance," drawled Ralph, brushing a lock of black hair out of his eyes and extending a huge hand to Lucy.

"Same here," said Lucy, grasping his hand and finding it pleasantly warm and strong.

"Take a seat," invited Hayden, setting cups on a Formica table. "How do you take your coffee?"

"Just black."

"Good for you. I can't resist adding cream, even though I shouldn't." Hayden patted his round little tummy.

Lucy sat down and shrugged out of her coat.

"Let me take that," said Ralph, hanging it up on a coat rack and then taking a seat beside her.

Hayden joined them, setting a plate of homemade blueberry muffins in the center of the table. Ralph helped himself to a huge one and passed the plate to Lucy, who shook her head and passed it along to Hayden.

"You're missing something special," said Ralph with a wink as he spread a generous pat of butter on his muffin. "Hayden makes great muffins."

"I wouldn't bother, except Ralph enjoys them so. And he never gains a pound, lucky devil."

"Not me," said Lucy, who had struggled to lose the twenty extra pounds she had gained when she was pregnant with Zoe and wasn't about to put back on. "I have to watch every calorie."

Ralph shrugged and reached for another muffin. "You know, you haven't made popovers in a dog's age," he said, turning to Lucy and indicating Hayden with a glance. "His popovers are even better than his muffins."

"I'm awfully glad he didn't," said Lucy, taking a sip of coffee. "I can never resist popovers."

"With homemade strawberry jam . . ." began Ralph.

"Stop!" yelped Lucy in mock distress. "I can't stand it! I guess I will have a muffin."

"So, Lucy," began Ralph, his tone now serious. "What do you think of all this business at the library?"

"I don't know what to think," admitted

Lucy. "I've only been to one board meeting."

"Heck of a meeting," he said, busying himself with buttering another muffin.

"Now, Ralph, don't discourage Lucy," said Hayden. "That's the first time we've ever actually had a murder — although I must admit we've come close a few times."

Lucy smiled at his joke. "I heard that the board was planning to fire Bitsy — is that true?" asked Lucy, nibbling on her muffin.

Ralph snorted and Lucy looked up sharply in surprise.

"I'm afraid Ralph doesn't have a very high opinion of some of the board members," explained Hayden. "But this is the first I've heard of any plan to fire Bitsy. I mean, I know Miss Tilley loathed her, but I don't think she could get the necessary votes. Staff changes take a unanimous vote. I wouldn't have voted to fire her, and neither would Chuck." He paused and looked at Lucy. "What about you?"

"No." Lucy's voice was firm.

"Maybe that's why she was killed," drawled Ralph.

Lucy's eyes met Hayden's. "Do you think one of the board members is the murderer?" she asked.

"It's crossed my mind," admitted

Hayden, "especially after Horowitz gave his little speech. What I can't figure out is when any of them had the opportunity. She must have been killed just minutes before you discovered her, and we were all together then."

"That's not quite true," Lucy reminded him. "It would only have taken a minute or two, you know, and both Ed and Gerald told Horowitz they left the group."

"What did I tell you?" demanded Ralph, pounding the table with his fist. "I told you my money was on Ed."

"Don't pay any attention to him," Hayden told Lucy. "He and Ed have never seen eye to eye. They have some . . . uh, philosophical differences."

"Right," agreed Ralph. "I'm civilized and he isn't."

Lucy smiled. "He is pretty crude, but that doesn't make him a murderer. And Gerald may be every bit the gentleman, but he was also away from the group for a few minutes."

Hayden nodded. "He said he went into the reference room to get the gavel for the meeting," he explained to Ralph.

"Ah-ha!" exclaimed Ralph. "But did either of you actually see him holding the gavel?"

"I didn't," said Lucy.

"Neither did I," said Hayden.

"Well, there's your suspect," announced Ralph.

"He's just joking, you know," Hayden hastened to tell Lucy. "I've been on that board for a long time. I know them all pretty well, and I honestly can't picture any of them shooting her. No matter what Ralph thinks, they really are a pretty decent bunch. They've all donated hours and hours of time to the library. I really think it must be something to do with Bitsy's personal life — after all, we knew very little about her except as the librarian."

"The problem with that is that she doesn't seem to have had any sort of a life at all. Kept herself to herself. At least, that's what her landlady said."

Ralph looked doubtful. "Everybody has some sort of private life. Everybody."

"Maybe we're overlooking the obvious here," said Hayden. "I finally got to read that article you and Chuck were talking about, about violence against librarians, and it said most of the violence was related to a robbery, either computers or some valuable artifact or other."

"But nothing was taken," protested Lucy.

"Maybe she discovered someone attempting a robbery. They killed her and then got frightened."

"That could be," agreed Lucy. "When I went downstairs all the art supplies were spilled, as if she'd been startled, or maybe even in some sort of struggle."

"That's awful," said Hayden, looking rather pale and turning his mug around in circles. "I didn't know that. Bitsy must have been terrified."

The three fell silent, staring at the table. Finally, Ralph voiced what they were all thinking.

"Winter in New England. It looks beautiful but it's brutal. And this winter's been especially bad. Right about now a lot of people are probably getting pretty desperate. The little they managed to save over the summer is gone and they don't have money for heating oil and food . . . and there are still a couple of months of cold weather ahead."

It was true, thought Lucy. Poverty was prettier in the country, where it was hidden away in the woods and tucked behind weathered clapboards, but it was every bit as terrible. She remembered the days when it had been a struggle to pay the bills and keep the children warm and fed. One winter, when there was no work, she and Bill had borrowed money from his folks. They were lucky. Without the elder Stones to help them out, they would have had to accept welfare and go to the food pantry in the cellar of the community church, like so many others. And now, welfare reform was literally leaving a lot of people out in the cold, forcing them to do whatever they could to survive.

"A robbery — that's probably what happened," she said, reluctant to pursue such a depressing subject further. A change of subject was definitely called for. "Now, before I go," she asked brightly, "where can I find a tankard?"

"Lucy was interested in those pewter tankards we had in the window," said Hayden. "She's looking for a gift for Miss Tilley."

"Not that I could have afforded those," Lucy hastened to add.

"They are extraordinary," Ralph told her. "A matched pair, impeccable provenance, superior craftsmanship, great age. They're worth every penny."

"I'm sure they are," said Lucy. "I had no idea pewter is so valuable. I guess I'll just send flowers."

"You could," agreed Ralph, with a shrug.

128

"Not that they'll last very long. The poor things will simply wither under her gaze."

"You're probably right," said Lucy, laughing. "Pewter would definitely be more durable."

"You can find nice pewter around here quite reasonably," offered Hayden. "I saw an interesting piece at that place — the Treasure Trove. I meant to go back and check it out."

"He's right," agreed Ralph. "Good stuff does turn up now and then around here. You know how the town got its name, don't you?"

"Tinker's Cove? Actually, I don't."

"It used to be a place where tinkers, you know, tinsmiths and pewterers and peddlers, spent the winter. They gathered here and worked all winter making the wares that they peddled to farms all over the state."

"I didn't know that," said Lucy.

"It means that every so often something really nice turns up. You know, that funny old ashtray of Grandpa's turns out to be a priceless, two-hundred-year-old porringer."

"I should be so lucky," said Lucy, rising to go. "I think I will check out the Treasure Trove."

"Happy hunting," said Ralph, shoving back his chair and standing up.

"Thanks for the coffee."

"The pleasure was all ours," said Ralph.

"We don't get to meet too many suspected murderers," agreed Hayden, holding her coat for her.

"Did I miss something?" asked Ralph.

"The police detective announced to the board members that I'm his prime suspect because I found Bitsy's body," said Lucy, blushing.

"I can't believe that," said Ralph.

"Of course not," said Hayden. "I was just joking."

"So was Lieutenant Horowitz — we happen to be old acquaintances," explained Lucy, pausing at the door. "At least I *hope* he was joking. Otherwise I'm in big trouble."

Nine

The Ogre guarded his treasure fiercely . . .

Lucy checked her watch when she left Hayden and Ralph and discovered she had at least an hour before she had to be home. She decided she might as well stop in at the Treasure Trove and see if they had any pewter.

The Tinker's Cove Treasure Trove, originally a gift shop built in the shape of a pirate's chest, had seen better days. It was located on Route 1A, the old state highway which used to be the major road to the coast. When the superhighway was built, however, tourists no longer had to spend hours creeping along on the old two-lane road and business declined. Once freshly painted every spring, the Treasure Trove's dark brown siding was now faded and peeling, and owner Frank Ford supplemented his shrinking stock of new items with so-called antiques and collectables sold on commission. When the yard sale was over, the Treasure Trove was only too happy to accept the leftovers.

When Lucy turned into the parking lot she didn't have any difficulty finding a space, even though only a small area had been plowed. Hers was the only car.

The dim afternoon light was already fading as she made her way carefully across the ice and clumped snow and reached for the doorknob. The door stuck and she had to yank hard before it finally opened. When she got inside, she was greeted with a welcome blast of heat from the coal stove Frank had constructed from an oil drum. Nobody seemed to be watching the store, so she began browsing among the cluttered counters, careful not to trip on any of the items that crowded the narrow aisles.

The place was an incredible jumble: pressed glass goblets and Depression glass plates were set on old cans of motor oil and stacks of *Life* magazines; boxes and boxes of old yellow *National Geographic* magazines; old-fashioned push lawnmowers and sets of rusty painted metal breadboxes and kitchen canisters; chipped plates and blue and green glass insulators from electrical poles. Nothing was organized — it was the sort of place where you could look for hours, finding worthless bits and pieces that brought back long-forgotten memories of childhood. Lucy picked up a clear glass pitcher painted with red and blue stripes and bright yellow lemons that was just like the one Aunt Helen had at the lake, except Aunt Helen's still had its matching tumblers, and re-membered Sunday afternoon visits and grown-up conversations that seemed end-less to a little girl who wanted to go swim-ming. She stroked a bright orange pillow crocheted from synthetic yarn that was just like the ones Mrs. Pilling had on her avo-cado green sofa, and recalled the day Mr. Pilling fell down dead in his yard from a stroke. His little beagle dog sat on the spot for days, waiting for Mr. Pilling to return.

Shaking her head to clear out the cobwebby images of days long past, Lucy picked up her pace and marched purpose-fully along, searching for the dull gray gleam of pewter. She poked in boxes of old pots and mismatched china and found a sugar bowl with no lid and a modern Scandinavian-style pitcher, rather dented. There were quite a few small trays, all modern and clunky-looking, engraved with "Our Daily Bread" in gothic letters. She was just about to give up, fearing it was getting awfully late, when she stumbled over a box of cans and tins containing screws and assorted hardware — clearly discarded from someone's garage or work-shop. She grabbed the corner of a glass display case to catch her balance and spotted a little tankard, hidden behind a plastic figure of Fritz the Cat.

The display case was locked, so she looked around for Frank. Not finding him, she gave a yell, and he came through the curtained doorway behind the sales counter. He was one of those thin, wizened people who never seemed to age, looking much the same at sixty as at forty. His hair was salted with gray and he was wearing his usual brown cardigan over a worn flannel shirt.

"Can I please see this old mug? The case is locked." One thing Lucy had learned from previous negotiations with Frank was never to use any word that might imply value to describe a desired object. It might be a pewter tankard but she would call it a mug, she resolved, as Frank bustled over with a bunch of keys attached to his belt with a chain.

She tapped her foot impatiently as he tried key after key, finally finding one that worked.

"This what you want?" he asked, lifting a

rather lumpy piece of amateur pottery.

"No, that metal one," said Lucy, pointing.

"Oh," said Frank, lifting it up and examining it. "This is nice."

"I just need something for pens and pencils — how much do you want for it?"

"I think this might be a genuine antique," said Frank, peering through his bifocals and stroking the white stubble on his chin. He glanced quickly at Lucy. "A hundred dollars."

"What?" Lucy made her eyes very wide, indicating her shock and surprise at this outrageous demand. "For that old thing? You're crazy. I wasn't planning on spending more than fifteen."

"I couldn't let it go for that," he said, shaking his head mournfully. "How about seventy-five?"

Lucy adjusted the strap of her shoulder bag and looked toward the door, as if she were preparing to leave. "Twenty-five, and that's my absolute limit."

"Fifty?" whined Frank.

"Done," snapped Lucy, whipping out her checkbook.

Leaving the store, Lucy encountered a woman struggling to carry a heavy cardboard box, and held the door for her. As if embarrassed, she gave a quick bob of her head in thanks and scuttled past.

Lucy noticed her turquoise jacket, a color that hadn't been fashionable for a number of years, and her boots, which were worn down at the heel. She guessed the poor thing was trying to raise a few dollars by selling her bits and pieces to Frank.

As she crossed the parking lot, carefully watching her footing in the waning light, she passed a big old sedan with patches of rust and a peeling vinyl roof. A heavy man with a big, bushy beard sat at the wheel and the back seat was filled with a squirming bunch of children.

She was opening the car door when she heard his voice. "I've had it with you," he growled. "Shut up, all of you!"

She glanced at him and he looked up at her. "What are you looking at?" he demanded.

She didn't answer, but ducked inside the car and shut the door. She started the engine, already feeling a little pang of guilt for spending so much money. While the car warmed up, she began unwrapping the tankard in order to take a closer look at it. Fifty dollars was more than she had planned to spend; she was already regretting the impulse that made her agree to such a high price. And as if to emphasize the waste, here, right next to her, were people who obviously had more need of that money than she did.

She turned to look at the crowded car once again, and saw the woman returning, still carrying the box. Apparently her things weren't even good enough for Frank. She had barely gotten back in the car before the man started the engine and, giving Lucy a glare, spun out of the parking lot at high speed, spraying bits of ice and gravel.

Who could blame him for being angry, thought Lucy. He and his family were wanting in the land of plenty and they weren't the only ones. Unfortunately, poverty was just about as common in Tinker's Cove as the rocks that lined the coast or the pine trees that stood in long-abandoned pastures. She remembered her conversation with Ralph and Hayden, and thought that a robbery was probably the reason for Bitsy's death.

With that thought came the discouraging realization that it was unlikely the murder would ever be solved. Without a motive, the police would only identify the murderer when, or if, something turned up in connection with another crime. A similar modus or someone willing to talk in exchange for a plea bargain.

Remembering the package in her hand, she took the little piece of pewter out of the crumpled newspaper Frank had wrapped it in. It was hard to see clearly in the dim light of late afternoon, but the tankard had a nice feel to it, she decided. It felt substantial in her hand but not too heavy. The shape was attractive, and even though pewter was a soft metal and dented easily, the straight sides were smooth. She wrapped her fingers around the handle and discovered they fit easily without pinching. Flipping it over, she examined the bottom and found it was smooth, with no identifying marks.

Lucy didn't know a great deal about antiques, but she felt confident that she had a good eye. She had visited museums and historic homes and studied the contents and frequently attended auctions, noting which items attracted the highest bids. And the more she studied the tankard, the happier she was with her purchase. She couldn't exactly say why, but something about the tankard made her suspect it was older and more valuable than she had originally thought.

Even so, thinking of the family in the car, she still felt guilty about spending such a lot of money so frivolously. She resolved to make a substantial contribution to the food pantry, and to go through the closets. The kids had plenty of outgrown but still serviceable winter clothes that could go to some less fortunate children.

Feeling somewhat better, she smiled as she flicked on the headlights and shifted into gear. Fifty dollars. It was a lot to her, but it was a far cry from the twenty thousand that Hayden had gotten for his matched pair.

What if, she thought as she pulled onto the dark road, she had discovered a truly valuable tankard, one that was worth thousands? It wasn't that ridiculous — after all, Ralph had said that good things turned up all the time, their value unrecognized until discovered by a knowledgeable collector or dealer. Maybe, she thought, hugging the happy thought to herself as she sped toward home, maybe she had found a real treasure at the Treasure Trove.

On Sunday afternoon Bill took the older kids to a benefit basketball game — the firefighters and police had teamed up against the teachers to raise money for a family that had lost their home when they tried to heat it with an old kerosene stove — and Lucy settled Zoe in front of the TV with a stack of videos and sat down at the computer to work on the gambling story. While she clicked away at the keyboard, she periodically looked away from the screen to admire the tankard. Here she was feeling guilty about spending fifty dollars for a gift for Miss Tilley, and at the same time Tinker's Cove residents were spending well over five hundred dollars per person, per year, on the state lottery.

At least she had something to show for her money — a useful and attractive object that she hoped would please her old friend. If she had spent that money on scratch tickets, she thought, all she would most likely have would be a pile of worthless cardboard.

It was odd, she thought, how quickly people had accepted the lottery. When she was a girl, she remembered, her mother had often criticized a neighbor who played the illegal numbers game. "It's a waste of money that could buy milk and bread for his children," she used to say. "He might as well throw it away."

It had been quite a surprise to Lucy when her mother began including lottery tickets in the children's Christmas gifts, and had also begun tucking them into birthday cards. What had happened to make her change her mind? After all, gambling was gambling, whether it was sponsored by the state or the mob. And with the chance of winning in the state's Big Big Jackpot at something like 55 million to one, the mob offered better odds.

Of course, the state lottery not only promoted their games with glossy advertising that promised wealth and happiness but it also was supposed to provide money for education. Funny, thought Lucy, giving a little snort, that taxpayers would resist a one or two percent increase in the property tax amounting to ten or fifteen dollars a year at the same time they would spend hundreds on the lottery.

"It's practically un-American not to play," she quoted the man from Gamblers Anonymous she had interviewed by telephone earlier that afternoon. "After all, Bingo supports the church and the lottery helps education. It's the new American Dream — you don't work hard to get rich, you just play the lottery."

Finishing up the story, Lucy picked up the tankard. She'd love to know how much it was worth. Had she lost money? Was it really worth only the fifteen dollars she had originally wanted to spend? Or was it a bargain at fifty? How could she find out? Tomorrow, she decided, she'd stop by the shop and ask Ralph to take a look at it. Maybe, she thought hopefully, she had a winner.

Ten

After they had been wandering in the woods for a very long time, Hansel and Gretel came upon a cottage made of gingerbread and candy.

On Monday morning, Lucy wasted no time in making good her resolution to make a donation to the food pantry. After leaving Zoe at the rec building for nursery school, she headed straight for the IGA. There, armed with the flyer that came in the Sunday paper, she took advantage of all the buy-one-get-one-free promotions, and filled her cart with boxes of pasta and jars of spaghetti sauce, cans of tuna fish and soup, and bags of rice and beans. All nutritious, filling stuff. She also bought a box of confectioner's sugar and a bag of conversation hearts; Valentine's Day was just around the corner, and she always made pink-frosted cupcakes trimmed with heart candies for the kids.

When she arrived at the community church, Lucy saw she wasn't the only one

making a delivery. Ed Bumpus was unloading a box from the back of his gargan-
tuan pick-up truck, a glossy black model
perched on oversized tires and trimmed
with lots of shining chrome. Lucy didn't
feel very friendly toward Ed — she hadn't
liked his attitude at the board meeting —
but she could hardly ignore a fellow
member.

"That's quite a truck you've got there,"
Lucy said, admiring the cab, which was
trimmed with a sun visor and topped with
a row of roof lights. A big, black Lab dog
was sitting inside.

"My wife says I'm no better than a little
kid — I gotta have my toys," he said,
hoisting the heavy box onto his shoulder.

"What have you got in there?" asked
Lucy, following him down the path to the
church basement.

"Moose," grunted Ed. "I give 'em one
every year."

"Did you shoot it yourself?" asked Lucy,
remembering the shotgun rack inside Ed's
truck.

Ed turned to face her, his puffy face even
redder than usual. "Usually, I do, but this
year, I struck out. My cousin got this one,
but don't tell the pastor, okay?"

"You've got a deal."

The basement door popped open as they approached, and the minister, Clive Macintosh, greeted them. He was new to the job, having arrived in Tinker's Cove only last summer.

"Well, well, what's all this?" he asked, rubbing his hands together.

"Moose. Wrapped and frozen and ready to cook," said Ed, dropping the box on a table with a thud and heading back out to get another.

"Terrific," said Clive, professing enthusiasm but looking somewhat doubtful.

"It's a Maine thing," Lucy hastened to reassure him. "Trust me — people will really appreciate it."

Clive looked at the box suspiciously. "How do you cook it?"

"Just like beef — it's not gamey," Lucy said, placing her bags of groceries on the table, too. She wished she'd thought to buy something a little more interesting. "These are just the usual nonperishables. Macaroni. Tuna. That kind of stuff."

"We can sure use it," said Clive, his eyes widening as Ed appeared with another box. "We're having a hard time keeping up with the demand. The committee members tell me it's the worst they've ever seen."

"It's the weather," said Lucy. "It's been

so cold that people are using more heating fuel than usual — that means there's less money for groceries."

"Well, we're certainly very grateful," said Clive as Ed set the box on the table.

"Think nothing of it. It's my pleasure," said Ed, panting a little from the exertion. "See you get this in the freezer, now."

"I will, and thanks again," said Clive as Lucy and Ed went through the door.

"He's a funny little guy," said Ed as they made their way up the walk to the parking lot.

"He's from some posh town in Connecticut," said Lucy. "I don't think they eat moose there."

"Can't be much of a place, then," said Ed, thoughtfully propping his elbow on the side of his truck. "Say, have you heard anything more about this Bitsy mess?" He wrinkled his forehead, jamming his bristly eyebrows together in concern. "Has that cop been botherin' you?"

"Oh, no." Lucy waved her hand dismissively. "That was just a joke. I've known him a long time. I'm not really a suspect."

"Wish I could say the same," muttered Ed. "He's been nosin' around my crew, gettin' in the way and askin' a lotta questions."

"He's just doing his job," said Lucy.

"Well, I wish him doin' his job didn't keep me from doin' mine."

Lucy nodded. She knew how much Bill, and most contractors, hated interference on their job sites. "Did you find out what he was asking about?"

"Lot of stupid stuff, if you ask me. I don't think he's got any more idea of who killed Bitsy than my dog here." He jerked his head toward the cab. "I heard you're kind of a detective yourself. Whadda you think?"

"Me?" Lucy didn't like the way Ed was staring at her with those beady eyes of his. She felt a bit like that poor moose, caught in the sight of one of his shotguns. "You heard the pastor — it's no secret how desperate people are this winter. I think Bitsy must have interrupted a robbery, something like that. Whoever did it is probably scared and laying real low. I don't think they're going to solve this anytime soon."

"Yeah," grunted Ed. "I think you're right." He opened the door to his truck and reached across the seat, giving the dog a pat on the head. "Say hi to Bill for me," he said, hoisting himself into the seat.

"Sorry, Lucy, but Ralph's not here," said Hayden, a few minutes later when Lucy

147

stopped by with the tankard. "He's over in Gilead, checking out an estate sale."

"That's too bad — I was hoping he could tell me if I had found a treasure or not," said Lucy, unwrapping the tankard and setting it on the table in the shop. "What do you think?"

"Very nice," said Hayden, examining the tankard. "I think it's lovely. Excellent craftsmanship. Nice patina. How much did you pay?"

"Fifty dollars."

He nodded approvingly. "That's a steal."

Lucy beamed with pride. "You really think so?"

"I do," affirmed Hayden. "But I ought to warn you — I'm no expert on pewter." He turned the tankard over and checked the bottom. "Interesting."

"What's interesting?"

"I don't want to get your hopes up, but you see how smooth it is? Josiah's Tankard, the one at the library, is like that, too. It means the piece was made in a mold. Later pieces were worked on a lathe and have finishing marks on the bottom. That means this tankard has quite a bit of age."

"Are you sure?" Lucy couldn't quite believe her luck.

"Yeah. Miss Tilley asked Ralph and me

to examine Josiah's Tankard a few months ago so we could write a description for the insurance policy. It was quite an experience — very hush-hush. After dark. The library was closed, of course. She even had a police officer standing by when we opened the case."

Lucy chuckled. "I can just imagine." She paused. "Then you think it's good enough to give to her as a present?"

"I'm pretty sure, but if you want to be extra safe, why not check with Corney? She has quite a nice pewter collection, you know."

"I didn't know," said Lucy, "but that's a very good idea. Thanks."

Lucy was hesitant to drop in on Corney unexpectedly, whom she barely knew, so she stopped first at the Quik-Stop to call. When she pulled the car up to the pay phone, she pulled in beside a dark blue Chevy sedan with its engine running. Climbing out of the Subaru, she noticed the sedan was occupied. Probably someone waiting for a companion who had dashed into the store.

She didn't waste time making the call — the temperature was well below freezing. Corney was home, testing a recipe, and said she'd love to see the tankard. Lucy was encouraged at her reaction. Not only would she learn more about the tankard, but she might be able to pick up some more information about Bitsy. Hurrying back to her warm car, Lucy glanced at the occupant of the Chevy.

He was hunched over the steering wheel and for a moment Lucy thought he might be sick. When she looked closer, however, she saw he was busily scratching away at a lottery ticket. Not a single ticket, she realized with a shock, but a stack of tickets at least an inch thick. He was so absorbed in this activity that he didn't even notice her.

Embarrassed, as if she had seen him doing something obscene, she quickly turned away and got into her own car. She started the engine and backed out too fast, skidding a bit on the icy parking lot. Regaining control of the car, she turned onto Route 1 and headed for Corney's place on Smith Heights Road, the most expensive section of Tinker's Cove, where enormous seaside mansions belonging to wealthy summer people clung to stony perches overlooking the sea.

How much did a stack of tickets like that cost, wondered Lucy as she drove along. Fifty dollars? A hundred dollars? Why would anyone spend that much money and then spend the morning sitting in a freezing parking lot? It didn't make any sense. You'd have to be crazy to do something like that. Or, she realized, possessed by an uncontrollable urge to gamble. An urge that was every bit as strong as an alcoholic's desire for a drink, or a drug addict's need for a fix.

Lucy shivered and made the turn onto Smith Heights Road. There, she was hardly warmed by the oceanfront view; cold surf was pounding the ice- and snow-covered rocks far below the road. A few black ducks were bobbing about in the waves and Lucy wondered how they could survive in such inhospitable conditions.

Corney said she wouldn't have any trouble finding the house, and she didn't. The jumbo-sized mailbox was clearly labeled "Corney Clarke Catering," but the topiary shrub in the shape of a chef was also an indication she was in the right place.

Corney's lengthy driveway was clear of snow right down to the blacktop and Lucy wondered how this was accomplished. Her own driveway contained a good deal of packed snow, despite Bill and Toby's best efforts. It had snowed practically every day since Christmas and shoveling walks and drives clear was a constant problem for most people, but apparently not for Corney.

Knocking on the door, Lucy noticed the Christmas wreath was already gone, replaced with a gilded wood pineapple. The pineapple, she knew, was a symbol of hospitality.

"Hi, Lucy, come on in," said Corney, opening the door. She was dressed in jeans and a sweater, topped with a spotless white chef's apron.

"Excuse my mess," she said, waving a hand at a breathtakingly attractive living room. Two white sofas draped with brightly colored quilts faced each other in front of a fireplace, moss green carpeting covered the floor, and brass accent pieces caught the fitful morning sunlight. The windows were filled with blooming narcissi and their sweet, heady scent filled the air. How come they didn't flop, wondered Lucy, who had started many a gravel-filled bowl of bulbs with the children. And how come they were all in bloom at the same time? All Lucy ever managed to grow were thin, straggly leaves that had to be propped up until they grudgingly produced a sickly blossom or two.

"Let's go in the kitchen," said Corney. "I'm baking and I need to keep an eye on things."

Lucy hesitated for a minute, reluctant to risk soiling Corney's floor with her boots. She needn't have worried, she realized; the hallway to the kitchen was paved with terra cotta tiles. She followed Corney on into the kitchen, where a huge, black, professional-style stove radiated a gentle warmth. A center island was covered with trays of scallop-shaped cakes and the aroma of butter and almonds was almost intoxicating.

"Boy, those smell good," said Lucy, climbing up onto an oak stool. Corney hadn't offered to take her coat, so she unzipped her parka and slipped her gloves into the pockets.

"They do, don't they?" agreed Corney, opening the oven and extracting a baking sheet. "Everyone loves madeleines and I think they're a nice alternative to those pink-frosted cupcakes everyone makes for Valentine's Day."

"I tried them once, but they stuck to the pan," admitted Lucy, refusing to think of the sugar and candy hearts sitting in her car, destined to be made into pink-frosted cupcakes.

"You have to butter the tins generously, and be sure to flour them, too," advised Corney. She gave the sheet a quick twist, and a dozen madeleines obediently popped out of their shell-shaped depressions. Corney slid them onto an antique wire rack and then faced Lucy. "So, what brings you here? I hope you don't want to talk about Bitsy — that was too awful. The sooner I can forget, the happier I'll be."

"I won't be able to forget until we know who killed her and why," said Lucy, somewhat self-righteously. She quickly added, "But I'm not here to talk about Bitsy. I wanted to ask your opinion about a tankard I bought. It's a gift for an old friend, and I want to be sure it's a good piece. Hayden told me that you collect pewter."

"I do," said Corney, waving her hand at an English pine dresser generously filled with assorted pieces of pottery and pewter.

"That's a lovely display," said Lucy.

"People often make a mistake with pewter," said Corney. "They'll think that just because a piece dates from the eighteenth century and costs the earth, that it belongs with their fine mahogany sideboard. It doesn't, of course. Mahogany really requires silver, and it makes pewter look drab. But here with country-style pottery and baskets and pine and oak — well, I think the result speaks for itself. It's spectacular."

"So it is," said Lucy, feeling rather humble as she produced the tankard and unwrapped it for Corney's inspection.

"Isn't that cute!" exclaimed Corney, taking it and looking it over. "I hope you didn't pay too much for it."

"Fifty dollars."

She nodded. "You didn't exactly get a bargain, but you didn't get rooked, either."

"Really?" Lucy was disappointed. "Hayden thought it might be quite old."

"Oh, no," said Corney, shaking her head. Even after a morning of baking, Lucy noticed, she looked neat and fresh and when she shook her head every hair fell right back into place. "See how the bottom is smooth? That means it's something called Brittania. It was kind of a new, improved pewter that was introduced in the nineteenth century. It was lighter, and instead of using molds the craftsmen could shape it on a lathe."

"But wouldn't that have left marks?"

"You'd think so, but the opposite is true. The very old pieces, the ones made in molds, have the marks. They're also much heavier."

155

"I must have misunderstood Hayden," said Lucy. "I thought he told me the opposite."

"I'm sure I'm right," said Corney, with a little nod. "I know my pewter."

"I'm sure you do," said Lucy, rewrapping the tankard. She felt her stomach rumble and realized she was hungry. Her eyes were drawn to the madeleines and she ran her tongue over her lips, wishing that Corney would ask her to stay for coffee. "These look so delicious," she said. "Did you use Cousin Julia's recipe?"

"All my recipes are original," said Corney, raising her eyebrows. "Besides, how would I have your cousin's recipe?"

Lucy laughed. "That's just what I call Julia Child."

"Julia Child is your cousin?" Corney was definitely interested.

"No, no," Lucy said and shook her head. "It's kind of an inside joke. When I was first married I used the Fannie Farmer cookbook a lot, and I happened to read the introduction by Fannie Farmer's niece. In it she calls Fannie Farmer 'Aunt Fannie'. After that, I started calling the book 'Aunt Fannie'. Then, when I got my Julia Child cookbook, I started calling that book

'Cousin Julia'." Noticing Corney's somewhat puzzled expression, Lucy finished lamely. "It's kind of stupid, I guess. In those days I hadn't done much cooking and it made me feel better to think I had a family of helpers."

"No, no. It's interesting," said Corney, who didn't sound interested at all. She started to pack the cooled madeleines in a tin lined with waxed paper.

Lucy sighed. It didn't look as if she was going to be offered a single one. "So you don't use cookbooks? All your recipes are original?" Lucy looked past Corney, at a row of strikingly beautiful amaryllis plants in full bloom that were sitting on a windowsill.

"They have to be — my reputation depends on it. I can't put someone else's recipes in my column."

"But isn't that difficult? I mean, most recipes are pretty similar. How can you come up with a new pie crust recipe, for example?"

"Oh, you add something to make it unique. A pinch of nutmeg." Corney waved her hands impatiently.

"I guess I really ought to be going," said Lucy, taking the hint and sliding off the stool. "So you start with a recipe by Aunt

Fannie, but you change it a little? Is that how it works?"

"Sometimes." Corney's face was getting flushed. "Sometimes I have an idea for something new, like my Cheesy-Zucchini bread."

"But that's really just a variation, isn't it?" They were standing by the door.

"Not at all." Corney practically spit out the words as she opened the door. "It's my own recipe. It's original. Nobody else makes Cheesy-Zucchini bread."

"Okay, if you say so," said Lucy, shrugging. This didn't seem to be the right time for a lengthy good-bye and she hurried to zip up her parka. "Well, thanks for your advice about the tankard." She gave a little wave and stepped through the doorway. The door thudded shut behind her, and the gilded pineapple rattled against the glass panes.

Lucy stood on the farmer's porch a minute to pull on her gloves. Then she walked to the car, wondering why Corney had been so brusque. You'd think the recipe police were watching what people cooked, or something. Good thing, thought Lucy as she pulled open the car door, that she hadn't told Corney about that zucchini variation for the Cheddar

Cheese Bread recipe that was printed right on the cornmeal box.

But as she drove down the snow-rutted streets to the rec center, where she was due to pick up Zoe, she wondered exactly how important this question of recipe authorship really was. She had certainly touched some sort of nerve with Corney.

And what if, she wondered, Bitsy had done the same thing? After all, Bitsy knew who took what books out of the library and didn't hesitate to jump to conclusions. If Corney had borrowed some cookbooks and then used the recipes in her column, claiming them as her own . . .

Lucy braked slowly at a stop sign and carefully turned the corner, pulling up in front of the rec building. She sat for a minute, tapping the steering wheel with her gloved hand.

"What am I thinking?" she muttered to herself. "That's just crazy," she added under her breath as she unstrapped the seatbelt and climbed out of the car. After all, nobody would kill somebody over a stupid recipe.

Eleven

The princess closed her eyes tight and kissed the ugly frog. When she opened her eyes she saw a handsome prince sitting in his place.

That evening, after the kids had settled down, Lucy joined Bill in the family room where he was exploring the Internet on the computer.

"That's disgusting!" she exclaimed, when she looked over his shoulder at the image on the screen. It was a rather grainy photograph of two women and a man engaged in sexual acrobatics.

"I think it looks like something we ought to try," said Bill, clicking the mouse. A dialog box appeared, inviting him to view more exotic pictures for the "low, low price" of nineteen dollars and ninety-five cents. All he had to do was type his credit card number in the box below.

He started to reach for his wallet, prompting a cry of protest from Lucy.

"Just teasing," he said, chuckling.

"It's a good thing I'm here to keep an eye on you," she said, settling herself on his knee and stroking his beard. "I had no idea this sort of stuff was in there." She let her head fall on his shoulder. "Can the kids find this stuff?"

"Sure."

Lucy watched as another picture gradually filled in the screen. It was a photograph of a naked woman in a dog collar on her hands and knees, lapping water from a bowl.

She clicked her tongue in disgust. "This explains a lot," she said.

"What do you mean?" Bill clicked the mouse and the picture disappeared, to be replaced by one of a bare-breasted dominatrix brandishing a whip.

"I couldn't understand why some of the library board members were giving Bitsy such a hard time about going on-line. Now I know why — can you imagine Gerald Asquith giving the go-ahead to something like this?"

"Oh, you never know," drawled Bill, clicking the mouse again. "Maybe Gerald enjoys a good spanking."

"Bill!" Lucy gave his hand a little slap. "Maybe you're the one who needs a spanking."

"Anytime," he said, winking and adding a growl.

"But seriously," began Lucy, "isn't it funny how you think you know people but you really don't?"

"What do you mean?" Bill gave the mouse another click to shut down the computer, and it began the usual series of squeaks and groans.

"Well, I've gotten to know some of the board members a little bit better and they're not quite what I expected. Take Hayden. I'd always kind of avoided him because I wasn't all that comfortable with his lifestyle, you know, the way he lives with Ralph. But I was over there the other day and they were terrific. I really like them."

"What were you doing over there?" Bill asked suspiciously, as he reached around Lucy to turn off the power switch.

"I saw something in the shop and I stopped in to ask the price — boy, that place is expensive! Anyway, after we'd established that I couldn't possibly afford anything in the place, Hayden gave me a cup of coffee."

"Hmph."

"Stop it. They're very nice. Both of them. You'd like them, too."

"I'm sure," said Bill. "But that doesn't

mean I have to approve of them."

"Whatever," said Lucy, not willing to argue. "And you know who I ran into at the food pantry? Ed Bumpus! He gave them a ton of moose meat."

"Ed's a good guy."

"Yeah, he is. What I can't figure out is why he's on the library board. He doesn't really seem like much of a reader."

"Ain't that the truth." Bill smiled. "He probably got finagled into it by somebody. He's one guy who can't say no."

"Not like Corney," mused Lucy. "She's one tough cookie."

"Really? I thought she was Ms. Bountiful, bringing the good life to one and all."

"Ms. Stingy is more like it," Lucy pouted. "I dropped in today while she was baking and she must have had hundreds of little cakes sitting there on her kitchen counter. Cooling, you know. Smelling absolutely divine. And it was getting on to lunch time and I was positively starving. I mean, actually drooling over the darned things, and do you think she gave me even one?" Lucy shook her head. "No way."

"Poor Lucy," said Bill, giving her a squeeze. "Come out to dinner with me on Valentine's Day at the Greengage Cafe and you can eat as much as you want. You can stuff yourself with crab ravioli and that terrific salad of theirs and all the tiramisu you can possibly eat."

"Are you serious?"

"Absolutely."

"Then you've got a date," said Lucy, giving him a long, lingering kiss.

The next morning, Lucy was humming as she fixed breakfast. After the kids departed, rushing out at the last minute to catch the bus, and Bill had given her a rather less perfunctory good-bye kiss than usual, she sat down at the computer.

"Mom! I want my bunny game!" complained Zoe.

"I want to check something — you can have the computer in a minute," said Lucy.

She leapfrogged her way through the World Wide Web and in a few minutes had e-mailed a message to S. Maddox Bailey, the curator of pewter at the Museum of Fine Arts in Boston. Confused by Hayden and Corney's conflicting advice about the tankard, she had decided to consult an expert.

She then played a few games of "Bunny Beware" with Zoe. She was surprised at how entertaining the game was; no wonder Zoe was addicted. After she finally won, she checked her e-mail and was disappointed to find no reply.

"I don't think this e-mail is all it's cracked up to be," she said, turning the computer over to Zoe.

Sitting down at the kitchen table, she unwrapped the tankard and examined it in the bright morning sunlight that was streaming through the windows. She could not find any evidence of finishing marks on the tankard's smooth bottom but just to be sure she used the magnifying glass she'd started keeping in the telephone book. Even then she could find no trace of any scratches.

According to Hayden, that meant the tankard was probably about the same age as Josiah's Tankard, which didn't have finishing marks, either.

Corney, on the other hand, had been quite certain that the tankard wasn't even made of pewter but of something called Brittania. How could she be so sure, Lucy wondered. That was the really irritating thing about Corney — she was such a know-it-all.

She set the tankard down on the oak table and got up to take something out of the freezer for dinner. When she turned back from the refrigerator she noticed that the kitchen was growing darker; the morning light was already being driven out by thick clouds. Her eyes fell on the tankard, and she smiled. The dimmer light suited it, she thought. It had a quiet, muted presence all its own that spoke of the long, gray winter, icy ponds, and the black, bare limbs of trees.

Corney must be wrong for once, thought Lucy. The tankard really was lovely. It would look wonderful on Miss Tilley's tavern table, filled with a few branches of winterberry. In early spring it would be perfect with pussy willow branches, then forsythia, and a bit later, lilacs. Come summer it could hold bright orange and red and yellow zinnias.

She carried it into the dining room, where she tugged open the bottom drawer of the big old pine dresser she used as a sideboard and began looking for a box and a bit of wrapping paper. There wasn't much there except for Christmas wrap; she would have to make do with plain white tissue paper.

That would be fine, she thought; somehow a gaudy pattern didn't seem quite right for Miss Tilley. Fortunately, she had saved a gift box that was just right for the tankard. She tucked it in and wrapped it, finishing the package with a narrow maroon ribbon.

Maybe it wasn't quite as fancy as something Corney would do, but it looked very nice, she thought, setting it on the table. She put away the wrapping things; it was time to think about lunch.

Passing through the family room to the kitchen she noticed Zoe had abandoned the computer; she was lining up her Barbies against the couch. Lucy gave the e-mail another try, but there was nothing.

Shivering, she checked the thermometer outside the kitchen window. Five degrees; now that the sun had disappeared the temperature was dropping. She went into the pantry for a can of soup and heard the furnace, down in the cellar, turn on.

She plopped the tomato soup into a pot and added water. As she stirred, she wondered how two experts like Corney and Hayden could have such different opinions on the tankard. Maybe Corney had been confused for some reason or other. If Josiah's Tankard didn't have finishing marks, and her tankard didn't either, they must both be about the same age.

While the soup heated, Lucy made sandwiches and poured two glasses of milk. Then she called Zoe for lunch, and ladled the soup into bowls.

"Careful, it's hot," she warned, sitting down opposite the little girl.

"I know, Mom. I'm not a baby."

"You're right, you're growing up," agreed Lucy, taking a bite of her sandwich. "What would you like to do after lunch? Do you want to invite one of your friends over to play?"

"Can I call Sadie?"

"Sure."

When they finished eating, Lucy checked the computer while Zoe made her phone call. This time, she had a response.

This is a question that I am frequently asked by beginning collectors. Oddly enough, the answer is different from what you might sensibly expect. Brittania, which is worked on a lathe, does NOT have finishing marks. Older pewter which was cast in a mold DOES have finishing marks. Hope this helps you.

So, Corney was right. She always was. Old pewter had finishing marks — that was what the curator at the museum had said. But hadn't Hayden told her that when he examined Josiah's Tankard a few months ago he had found no finishing marks?

Stunned, Lucy slid into a chair. Could that be right? Had she somehow misunderstood? No, she clearly remembered Hayden telling her that old pewter, like Josiah's Tankard, had a smooth bottom.

Lucy felt her chest tighten. This was important. She drummed her fingers on the computer table. If Hayden was right, Josiah's Tankard was a fake. It had to be a relatively modern reproduction that had been substituted for the original.

Was that why Bitsy had been killed? Lucy found herself on her feet, heading for the phone. What if Bitsy had discovered the theft? That could be the motive for her murder. She didn't even need to know that the tankard was a fake to be a danger, realized Lucy, pushing open the swinging door to the kitchen. Simply suggesting that the tankard could be sold to raise money would have put the thief in jeopardy.

After all, only a few people had access to the tankard. Once the theft was discovered it would be easy enough to figure out who had taken it.

Zoe looked up as her mother approached the telephone. "Sadie's not home," she said, shaking her head sadly and replacing the receiver on its hook.

Lucy didn't reply, but started to snatch

the phone, determined to call Horowitz. Suddenly, her hand in midair, she stopped. Hayden, she thought, feeling her heart sink. Oh, no. It had to be Hayden. He had told her himself that he had been the last person to handle the tankard.

But he'd said the examination had been supervised. Miss Tilley had been there, probably a few others besides. And a policeman. Lucy gladly seized on the idea. Hayden couldn't have taken it then. He had been watched far too closely. And besides, she thought, her mind whirling, the substitution could have been made earlier.

It must have been, Lucy realized. In fact, it could have been switched anytime in the last hundred years. She heaved a great sigh of relief and started once again to pick up the phone. Just then it rang.

"Lucy — Julia here."

"Julia? Oh, Miss Tilley! I didn't recognize your voice."

"Lucy," she began, her voice more quavery than usual. "Something terrible has happened."

"Are you all right?" Lucy's first thought was that the old woman had had an accident. "Have you fallen?"

"No, no. I'm fine," Miss Tilley said, impatiently brushing away her concern. "It's the tankard. It's gone."

"Gone?"

"Gone. Stolen. When I got to the library I found the case smashed to smithereens."

"Oh, no." Lucy tried to absorb this new information. "When did this happen?"

"I don't know. I just discovered it."

"Are you in the library now?"

"Yes."

"Who's with you?"

"No one."

Lucy was suddenly fearful for her elderly friend, bird-thin and frail, possibly alone with a thief in the closed and deserted library.

"I'll be right there," she said.

Twelve

*Snow White took a bite of the poisoned apple
and fell to the ground.*

Getting right there seemed to take forever.
Lucy had to pry Zoe away from her Barbies
and hustle her into her outdoor clothes.
Then she had to throw on her own parka
and boots, and scrape the ice-covered windshield of the car. All the time she was busy
with these frustrating details, she was dis-
tracted, worrying about Miss Tilley. What if
the thief was still in the library? And why had
she called her — why hadn't she called the
police?

When Lucy finally pulled up in front of
the library, she automatically began to un-
strap Zoe from her booster seat. Then she
stopped and refastened the seatbelt.
There was no way she was going to take
her little girl into a potentially dangerous
situation.

"I'm just going to run in for a minute,"

she told Zoe. "Don't you dare move, okay?"

"Okay, Mommy." Zoe's eyes were big and round; like a little fawn, she was alert to her mother's unease.

"I'll be right back," promised Lucy, closing the car door and locking it.

She dashed up the library steps, observing the fact that the big oak door showed no sign of a break-in. But when she entered the vestibule, she couldn't help gasping when she saw the smashed glass case. The recessed alcove that had contained Josiah's Tankard was now empty, filled only with a few shards of broken glass.

Proceeding on into the library proper, Lucy found Miss Tilley sitting glumly at the circulation desk.

"Have you called the police?" asked Lucy.

"Of course," snapped Miss Tilley. "What do you take me for? An idiot?"

"Why aren't they here?"

"I don't know. They said there was some sort of emergency and they'd get here as soon as they could. You got here pretty quickly — I hope someone is keeping an eye on that sweet little girl of yours."

"Actually, I left her in the car," said Lucy.

"You did? What were you thinking? Go and get her immediately!"

"I thought you might be in some sort of danger," said Lucy, defending her actions. "I thought she'd be safer in the car."

"Well, there's no danger here. I wouldn't have called you except for the fact that they're taking so long to get here. I was getting bored."

"I see that," said Lucy, biting her tongue. "I'll go and get Zoe now."

As she hurried back to the car, Lucy figured it must have taken her at least twenty minutes to reach the library. That was a long time to wait for help, considering that the police station was just around the corner. What could have happened, that they couldn't have responded more quickly?

Taking Zoe by the hand, Lucy hurried back up the steps. In the vestibule, the little girl planted her feet, stopping suddenly.

"It's broken," she said, pointing at the glass case with her pink mittened hand.

"I know. A bad person broke it and took what was inside."

"A bad boy?"

"Maybe," said Lucy, unable to resist smiling. "We don't know who did it."

Lucy pushed open the interior doors.

"That's my girl," cooed Miss Tilley. "If you pick out a book, I'll read it to you."

"Go ahead," said Lucy, giving her an encouraging shove in the direction of the children's section. "I wonder what's holding up the police?" she said, turning toward Miss Tilley.

"That's what I'd like to know," fumed Miss Tilley.

Lucy had expected her old friend to be distraught and upset, perhaps even ill with shock, but Miss Tilley seemed to be just plain mad. Her jaw was set and her teeth were clenched, and she was drumming impatiently on the desk with her knobby, blue-veined hand.

"When did you discover the theft?" asked Lucy, unzipping her parka.

"When I got here this morning — it must have been about eleven-thirty. We finally got permission from the police to reopen — it certainly took them long enough to look for that gun or whatever they were doing in here. I called Gerald this morning and he told me." The old woman cackled. "I don't think he was planning on calling me. He made a great point of telling me that I didn't need to concern myself about the library and he had found a temporary

175

librarian. Well, I wanted to make sure the police had left things in good order. I had planned to do some errands with Rachel anyway, so I had her drop me off here and she went on to the IGA.

"Of course, I noticed the theft as soon as I opened the door. I tried to call her back but she had already gone. So I called the police. And you."

Lucy reached out and patted her hand. "I'm glad you called me. I know this must be very upsetting for you."

"Of course it is." Miss Tilley's expression seemed to imply that Lucy was mentally deficient. "I feel a great responsibility for the safety of the tankard. It represents the history of our town."

Lucy decided to keep her suspicion that the tankard was not genuine to herself for the time being. "It seems an odd thing to steal," observed Lucy. "Is it worth a lot?"

"Similar tankards have gone for twenty-five thousand or more at auction," said Miss Tilley. "But I don't imagine it's the sort of thing you can get quick cash for like a TV or a computer or something like that."

"That's true," agreed Lucy, a little surprised at her old friend's understanding of criminal behavior. "Can I make you some tea or something?"

"Might as well. It doesn't seem as if the police are in any hurry." Miss Tilley was beaming at Zoe, who was climbing up onto a chair beside her. "You picked one of my favorites, you clever girl . . . 'Blueberries for Sal'."

Lucy went off to Bitsy's office to heat up some water and when she returned with two steaming mugs she found that Lieutenant Horowitz had arrived. Much to her surprise he had only one officer in tow, and was unaccompanied by the usual crowd of crime scene technicians. He was carrying a small bundle and placed it in front of Miss Tilley.

"I think we've solved your robbery," he said. "Would you take a look at this and identify it if you can?"

Miss Tilley unwrapped the brown paper bag with trembling hands and drew out a tankard encased in a plastic bag. "This is Josiah's Tankard," she said, emitting a shaky sigh of relief. "This is wonderful. I can't tell you how pleased I am."

Lucy gave her a big smile and a hug. "Do you mind if I look at it? I've never seen it up close."

Receiving a nod of permission from Miss Tilley, Lucy picked up the tankard and placed it under the desk lamp. Examining it through the clear plastic, Lucy could see the primitive design of the tree and bird, and the crude date and letters. The tankard appeared to be authentic, but when Lucy examined the bottom she found it was smooth, just like the tankard she had bought. It also seemed lighter than she would have expected, given the shape and size of the piece. "It's lovely," she said, handing it back to Miss Tilley.

"Well, that's that," said Horowitz. "Crime solved."

Just then the double doors burst open and Rachel rushed in, breathless from running up the stairs.

"What's going on?" she demanded, panting to catch her breath. "I saw the police car outside . . . and the broken glass . . ."

"Everything's under control," Lieutenant Horowitz informed her.

"The tankard was stolen," added Lucy.

"But it's been recovered," concluded Miss Tilley, giving the tankard a proprietary little pat.

"Well then, if the lieutenant has no objections, I think I ought to get you home," Rachel told Miss Tilley. "You've had quite a morning."

"No objections," said Horowitz, as Rachel helped Miss Tilley to her feet. "We have to keep the tankard for evidence for the time being, but I give you my personal promise that it will be returned to the library as soon as possible."

"I understand," agreed Miss Tilley, slipping her arms into the sleeves of the coat Rachel was holding for her. "Besides, it wouldn't be safe here until we have repaired the case."

She then took the younger woman's arm and made her shaky way to the door. The morning had definitely taken a toll on her, thought Lucy.

But when she removed her coat and Zoe's from the coat rack, preparing to leave, Horowitz stopped her.

"I'd like a word with you, Mrs. Stone," he said, causing Miss Tilley and Rachel to glance at her curiously.

"I'm afraid you can't stay here," said Miss Tilley. "I have to lock up."

"You can just give the key to me," said Horowitz.

"I'm afraid that won't do," said Miss Tilley, standing her ground. "I am responsible for locking the library."

"All right," said Horowitz, taking Lucy's elbow and steering her through the doorway. He stopped on the steps and they waited while Miss Tilley locked the door with trembling hands. He gave the officer a nod, and the young trooper gave Miss Tilley his arm. Slowly, the trio descended the steps toward Rachel's car.

A gust of wind hit them and Zoe huddled close to her mother, wrapping her arms around Lucy's hips. Lucy shivered and turned up her collar, waiting for Horowitz to speak. She sensed from the way he was tapping his foot on the stone step while he waited for Miss Tilley to get out of earshot that he was angry with her but she didn't understand why.

"I warned you not to mess around in this investigation," he began, glaring at her.

"I haven't been," said Lucy, her eyes opening wide with surprise. "Really."

He waved the plastic-wrapped tankard at her. "So why were you asking Hayden Northcross about this?"

"I was only asking his advice. I wanted to buy a tankard as a gift for Miss Tilley."

"And was he helpful?"

"Not really. He gave me the wrong information." Lucy paused. "That's not the real Josiah's Tankard."

"What?" Horowitz looked at her skeptically.

"It's a fake."

"Hayden told you that?"

"No, but he was wrong," said Lucy, struggling to keep her teeth from chattering in the cold. "It doesn't have any finishing marks on the bottom."

"That means it's a fake?"

"According to the curator of pewter at the Museum of Fine Arts."

"This is very interesting," said Horowitz. His breath made a cloud in front of his face.

"I think this might have something to do with Bitsy's murder," suggested Lucy, wrapping her arms around Zoe.

"Oh, yes. Yes, it does." Horowitz was rapidly tapping his foot.

"Well, I don't know anything about that," said Lucy, defending herself. "I was only trying to find out if a little tankard I bought in a junk shop was worth anything."

"And was it?"

"No." Lucy shook her head and picked up Zoe, hugging her tightly. "Just about what I paid for it."

"Not like this one. It may be a fake, but it cost two people's lives."

"Two lives?" Lucy's face was white. "Bitsy and who?"

"Hayden Northcross. He shot himself this morning."

"Oh, no!"

"It looks like he murdered Bitsy. The suicide gun is the same caliber as the murder weapon but we still have to test it to be sure."

"Oh, my God. Hayden. I can't believe it," said Lucy. Zoe was suddenly very heavy in her arms and she let her slide back down to the ground.

"I'm guessing he switched the tankards a while ago. Something like that isn't easy to fence, but as an antiques dealer he was in the perfect position to sell it."

"He told me he was asked to examine it a few months ago." Lucy's voice was flat and expressionless. She didn't want to believe her earlier suspicions about Hayden were true.

"He may have taken it then. Or earlier. It doesn't matter. I think Bitsy discovered the switch, and that's why he killed her. Then you come along, asking questions about tankards and he panics and offs himself."

"Are you saying he killed himself because of me?" Lucy was astonished.

"I am." Horowitz nodded his head sharply and glared at her. "If you hadn't gone around asking questions you had no business asking, he'd be alive today and I'd have Bitsy's murderer instead of a whole lot of guesses and suppositions and a case that will never be closed."

"I had no idea . . ."

"That's right. You have no idea. You just go poking around, sticking your nose in places you have no business. Well, I'm warning you. The next time you start messing around in one of my investigations I won't hesitate to slap you with charges of obstruction. So from now on you better just mind your own business, okay? And as for your suspicions about that tankard you'd better keep them to yourself. Understand?"

Horowitz was angry, but his gray face didn't pick up any color. The long lines between his nose and mouth simply hardened, like fast-setting concrete.

"Okay," said Lucy meekly.

She watched as Horowitz snatched the tankard and marched down the steps and climbed into the cruiser, giving the officer behind the wheel a nod. He accelerated, driving off in a cloud of exhaust vapor.

"I'm cold, Mommy," whined Zoe. "Let's go."

Moving on automatic pilot, Lucy descended the steps, carefully holding Zoe's hand so she wouldn't slip on the ice. She helped her get settled in the booster and then climbed into the driver's seat, turning on the ignition and pushing the heat to high.

She didn't put the car into gear, though; she just sat there, sorting through her emotions. Hayden was dead. It was all wrong. He wouldn't have killed himself, and he certainly wouldn't have killed Bitsy.

She felt a surge of anger. How could Horowitz accuse her of driving Hayden to kill himself? She hadn't had anything to do with it. Or had she? A sense of guilt stole over her. Maybe she had blundered onto something, asking questions about the tankard. Clutching the steering wheel, she rested her forehead on her hands.

"Mommy! Let's go!" demanded Zoe from the back seat.

She was right, thought Lucy. This wasn't accomplishing anything.

"In a minute," she said, rummaging in her shoulder bag for the cell phone she carried in case of emergencies. She punched in the number for *The Pennysaver* office.

"Ted? It's Lucy."

"Hi, Lucy. You got that story on gambling for me?"

"Uh, no," said Lucy. "I do have something, though. Have you heard about Hayden?"

"Hayden Northcross? No. What?"

"He's killed himself."

"No way — are you sure of this?"

"Horowitz just told me."

"Thanks, Lucy. I'll get right on it."

Lucy pushed the button to end the call and replaced the phone. Then she pulled away from the curb, not quite sure where she was going.

Lucy took Zoe to McDonald's, partly to reward her for being such a good girl all morning and partly because she didn't want to go home. The bright colors and shiny surfaces of the fast-food restaurant seemed preferable to the quiet house.

Zoe chomped on her cookies and slurped down a cup of hot chocolate, but Lucy found that once she had her apple pie she couldn't eat it. She sipped her coffee instead, trying to put the morning's events in perspective.

Hayden was dead. She still couldn't believe it. She didn't want to believe it. She liked Hayden. She wouldn't have hurt him for the world. She felt a flush of anger and resentment against Horowitz. How could he think she would have pushed Hayden into a corner, leaving him no option but suicide?

And she didn't believe for one minute that Hayden had killed Bitsy. After all, he had genuinely seemed to like her. Lucy ran a finger up and down the side of her coffee cup. This just didn't add up. After seeing Hayden and Ralph together, she was convinced Hayden would never have killed himself. Through the years she had learned something about human relationships, and she would have bet the house that they were truly devoted to each other. Horowitz was definitely on the wrong track.

She turned the empty Styrofoam cup in circles on the Formica table and watched Zoe pop the last cookie into her mouth. More than anything she wanted to get to the bottom of this and Horowitz wasn't going to stop her. She wanted to know who killed Bitsy, and Hayden. Because the more she thought about it, the surer she was that Hayden hadn't killed anyone. Not Bitsy, and not himself.

Noticing that Zoe was finished, Lucy crumpled up the food wrappers and squeezed them into a tight ball. Then, rebelliously leaving the tray on the table instead of carrying it over to the trash container, she took Zoe's hand and led her to the car.

Thirteen

The Seven Dwarves placed Snow White's body in a glass casket and covered it with flowers.

The reference room was the same as always. The rich patina of the pine paneling glowed softly in the light of the wall sconces, the portrait of Henry Hopkins glowered down from above the unused fireplace, and the big oak table and captain's chairs were in their usual place. But the group of directors gathered at an emergency meeting the next morning were stunned and shocked.

Or doing a good job of appearing that way, thought Lucy, as she studied the faces of her fellow directors.

"First Bitsy and now Hayden," said Corney. "I can hardly believe it."

"When I heard the news on my car radio last night I nearly went off the road," said Chuck. He shook his head slowly. "I just don't understand it."

Lucy wished she knew a little more

about Chuck. He seemed like such a nice guy; she wondered if he really was.

Corney certainly thought he was. She had reached across the table and was giving his arm a consolatory squeeze. Her expression was one of sincere sympathy. Oh please, thought Lucy.

"It's most distressing," agreed Miss Tilley in a matter-of-fact tone. "But at least the tankard has been recovered."

That damn tankard, it seemed to Lucy as she studied the old woman's face, was far more important to Miss Tilley than Bitsy and Hayden's lives.

"He was always an odd duck, if you get my drift," said Ed, hoisting one of his bristly gray eyebrows and twisting his mouth into a leer. He was nervously jiggling his leg and fidgeting with his big, callused hands. He looked around abruptly. "Where the hell's Gerald? I don't have all morning, you know. I've got work to do."

"He's making copies," volunteered Lucy. She'd liked Ed when she ran into him at the food pantry but today she wanted to scream at him, telling him to get out and leave the meeting if he had such important business. She didn't want to hear his nasty innuendos about Hayden, or his sexist comments about Bitsy. They were dead and they deserved a minimum of respect and a few minutes of his time. She didn't say anything, however, but sat quietly, twisting her wedding ring round and round her finger. She looked up when Gerald bustled into the room and began distributing copies of the agenda.

"I guess you've all heard the news," he began. "Our fellow director, Hayden Northcross, took his own life yesterday. I spoke with the police officer in charge of the investigation, Lieutenant Horowitz, and he told me that he believes Hayden was responsible for Bitsy's murder, also." His voice faltered, but he cleared his throat and continued. "Apparently overcome by remorse, he committed suicide."

For what seemed to be a very long time, no one said anything. The directors' eyes were downcast; they all appeared to be studying their agendas intently. Finally, Corney broke the silence.

"Hayden killed Bitsy?" she asked. "That's incredible."

"Did the lieutenant give you any idea *why* he killed Bitsy?" asked Chuck.

"No." Gerald sighed. "He wouldn't give me any details, just told me that as far as he is concerned the case is closed."

There seemed to be a lessening of tension in the room, thought Lucy, as if a general sigh of relief had been expressed.

"I don't suppose we'll ever know," volunteered Ed. "So let's get on to item two, if you don't mind."

"I mind," said Lucy, surprised to hear her own voice. "Two people are dead, two people who cared about this library. Aren't we going to do something in their memory?"

"Absolutely." Gerald nodded. "I'm open to any suggestions you may have."

"The obvious thing would be to name the new wing after them. We could announce it at the dedication ceremony," offered Lucy.

"That could turn out to be embarrassing," cautioned Chuck. "After all, we don't know all the details yet."

"I quite agree," said Miss Tilley in a firm voice. "I understand Bitsy's family is planning a memorial service in Massapequa. I suggest we send flowers. I don't know if plans have been made yet for a service for Hayden, but we could also send flowers when it is announced."

"I think that's the best course of action, at least for the time being," said Gerald. He looked around the table and everyone nodded agreement.

"Now that that's out of the way, can we move on?" demanded Ed.

Gerald looked at him sharply, then consulted his agenda. "The next order of business is the reopening of the library. I would like to propose we hire Eunice Sparks as interim librarian — I have her resumé here and, as you can see, she is well-qualified and I can personally recommend her. She can start immediately, and I propose we reopen on Monday."

Gerald passed out copies of the resumé and the directors bent their heads over them.

"There's no question that she's a qualified librarian," observed Miss Tilley. "However, in a situation like this it might be preferable to have someone who is familiar with our library. I would be more than happy to serve in the interim, on a volunteer basis."

"We certainly appreciate your offer," said Gerald, quickly. "However, it would not be fair to take advantage of your generosity. You are far too valuable to the library as a member of the board, and as you know, it is against our policy to include employees as board members." He had expected this reaction from Miss Tilley and had prepared for it, realized Lucy, impressed despite herself.

Heads bobbed around the table; the others were relieved to have this matter dealt with so neatly. Ed shifted restlessly in his seat.

"There is just one remaining matter and then I'll adjourn the meeting," said Gerald. "We now have a vacancy on the board, and we also need to find a permanent librarian. We already have a nominating committee to suggest new board members — it includes me, Chuck and," here he paused before adding, "Hayden."

"I'll take his place," offered Lucy.

"Any objections?" Gerald looked around the table. "Very well then."

"I'll head the search committee for a new librarian," volunteered Chuck.

Predictably, Corney also volunteered.

"I suggest Miss Tilley," said Ed. "She knows the job better than anyone."

"That's settled then," said Gerald, bringing down his gavel.

But he was wrong, thought Lucy, as she buttoned her coat. Nothing was settled at all.

Fourteen

Then one day, Bambi's mother told him that hunters had come to the forest.

After the meeting Lucy hurried out to her car. She had no inclination to linger and chat with the other board members. She no longer felt comfortable in the library; she just wanted to get away. When she pulled open the door to the car, yanking hard because it was stiff in the cold, she spotted a foil-wrapped package she had left on the back seat and paused.

With a sinking heart she remembered she had another errand — she had planned to make a condolence call at Ralph's, bringing a sour cream coffee cake she had baked especially for him.

She was tempted to skip it but her conscience got the better of her and she drove across town to the house he had shared with Hayden. She paused before knocking on the door, wondering briefly if she could just leave the cake. Instead, she raised the knocker and pounded it home. It was an ornate knocker, hanging on one of a pair of carved oak doors, with huge black wrought iron hinges and a dangling iron circle instead of a traditional doorknob. That was because Ralph and Hayden had converted a church, abandoned when the Methodists joined the Congregationalists to create the Tinker's Cove Community Church, into a home.

Hearing the click of the lock being unlatched, Lucy braced herself to face Ralph. Even so, she was shocked when the door finally opened, revealing his ravaged face. The dark shock of hair that had reminded her so much of the young Gregory Peck hung limp and greasy today and there were deep hollows under his cheekbones.

"I wanted you to know how sorry I am about Hayden," Lucy began. "I baked this coffee cake for you."

"Thanks." Ralph took the foil-wrapped package and stood looking at it. "Would you like some coffee?" he finally asked. "I know I should eat but I can't face sitting at the table alone."

"Of course," said Lucy, swallowing hard. It would be easy enough to make an excuse and flee back to the comfort and security of home, but that would mean abandoning Ralph to his grief and loneliness. "I'd love some coffee," she said.

Ralph led her through the spacious living room, formerly the sanctuary of the church, which was now furnished with Victorian sofas and Oriental carpets. They went downstairs, where the old church hall now served as an elegant dining room and the spacious kitchen had been modernized with top-of-the-line appliances and cabinets. While Ralph filled the coffee pot, Lucy sat herself at the huge antique refectory table and sliced the cake.

"This is good," said Ralph, taking a huge bite and showering brown sugar and nuts onto the table. Embarrassed, he brushed them away. "I haven't eaten much, lately."

"I wanted to make popovers for you — I remembered you saying how much you like them — but they didn't come out."

He nodded. "That happened to Hayden, too, until he started using four eggs." He sighed, and his voice quavered. "He swore by the Moosewood Cookbook."

"That must have been it," said Lucy, content to talk about comforting trivialities. "I only used two. Fannie Farmer can be a bit stingy with eggs."

"Yankee thrift." He swallowed hard. "We

used to argue about it. I said it was a result of the rocky soil and the hard climate. Hayden said it was just meanness of spirit."

"There was nothing mean about Hayden — he had a generous spirit," said Lucy, accepting a cup of fragrant Kenyan blend. "It must have been an awful shock."

"It was — it still is," said Ralph, sitting down opposite her and spooning sugar into his cup. "I know he's gone — there's no doubt about that — but somehow I can't believe it. I keep expecting him to walk in and say it was all a mistake."

"That's natural. Everybody feels like that. It's unthinkable, so it can't be true." She reached out and patted his hand. "After a while, when you feel up to it, maybe you could try one of those support groups that help you cope with loss."

Ralph snatched his hand away. "I don't know how welcome I'd be, given the circumstances." He paused. "I think I have to do this my own way."

Lucy chewed her cake thoughtfully. He was right, of course. As a homosexual grieving the loss of a same-sex partner, he would certainly be the odd man out with the widows and widowers. "It must be terrible," she said, thinking of how lost she would be without Bill.

"It is. It's indescribable. It hurts physically, you know. I feel like I've been hit by a truck and had my insides ripped out. Even breathing hurts. And the worst part is what the police said. That he killed himself. That he killed Bitsy. That can't be true."

Lucy looked around the kitchen, the kitchen that had been Hayden's. Gleaming copper pots hung from a rack above the stove. A row of potted herbs stood on the windowsill above the sink. Cookbooks were tucked away, yet ready at hand, in a shelf built into the work island. It was so like Hayden, she thought. Simple. Attractive. Practical.

"I don't think anybody who knew him believes the police theory," said Lucy.

"I'll never believe he would hurt Bitsy," insisted Ralph. "He'd never hurt anybody — especially not me. We had all kinds of plans for the future — we'd just bought tickets for a cruise next month. Not to mention the plans we had for the business, and the house. We were going to set up a website and buy new carpet and redo the bathroom. Someone who's going to kill himself doesn't sit up half the night looking at wallpaper books, does he?"

"I don't think so," said Lucy.

"And that business about stealing the tankard — that's nonsense. He wouldn't do that — he has . . ." Ralph's voice broke as he corrected himself. "He *had* too much respect for antiques. They were his life. He would never do something like that." He shrugged. "He didn't need to. The business is successful — we were making plenty, believe me."

"What do you think happened?"

"I don't know." He ran his fingers through his hair and propped his elbow on the table, resting his head on his hand. "I think it had something to do with the library. First Bitsy and now him." He picked at a crumb of brown sugar. "I should never have gone away that day — I blame myself. We were both going to go to an estate sale in Lewiston, but he said he had some library business he had to clear up. Told me to go to the sale without him. 'Make a killing' he said. Those were his last words to me."

Lucy felt rotten when she left Ralph. She felt completely inadequate in the face of such raw grief. As a mother, she was used to patching up boo-boos with Band-Aids, giving a kiss and making it all better. There

199

was nothing she could do to help Ralph — her healing powers could not cure his pain.

"What's the matter, Lucy? You look as if you lost your best friend!" exclaimed Sue, who was just leaving the recreation building when Lucy arrived to pick up Zoe.

"I just took a cake to Ralph," explained Lucy. "He's having a real hard time."

Sue was serious. "We're all going to miss Hayden. He was some character." She sighed. "I was going to ask his advice about slipcovering the couch. I was going to have him over for lunch one day — he was always fun, and he would have had some terrific ideas." She tucked her glossy black hair behind her ear. "Say, do you have any plans for lunch today?"

"Nothing beyond peanut butter and jelly and chicken noodle soup," admitted Lucy.

"Come on over to my house. We can cheer each other up."

"Thanks," said Lucy, smiling for the first time that day. "I'll get Zoe and I'll be right over."

Sitting at the table in Sue's gleaming, streamlined kitchen, Lucy thought how nice it was that she and Sue were able to spend more time together. After Sue had started the day-care program in the community center she had been working full-time, determined to make the project a success. Thanks to her determination and hard work, skeptical town meeting voters were now convinced of the once controversial center's value, and generally approved annual funding without a murmur of opposition. Now convinced that the center's future was secure, Sue had recently cut back her hours and only worked mornings.

"I want to have some time for myself," she had told Lucy. "I want to be able to take a walk, or curl up with a good book, or take an afternoon nap. That's not a crime, is it?"

"Certainly not," agreed Lucy, who had fallen into the habit when the children were little and always seemed to find herself growing sleepy after lunch.

"So, tell me what you think about these sudden deaths," said Sue, interrupting her thoughts and giving her a handful of silverware to set the table. Zoe was happily ensconced in the living room with a sandwich and a pile of carrot sticks, watching a Disney video.

"I don't know what I think," confessed Lucy. "The police theory is that Hayden stole the tankard some time ago and replaced it with a fake. Bitsy discovered the substitution and confronted him and he killed her. Overcome with remorse, he killed himself."

"But you don't believe that," said Sue, tucking a covered dish into the microwave.

Lucy thoughtfully laid a fork down on the table. "No. You knew Hayden better than I did. Do you think he was a thief? That he would murder Bitsy? I just can't believe it."

"Me, either," agreed Sue, ripping apart a head of lettuce to make a salad.

"I do think this all has something to do with the tankard." Lucy folded a napkin and placed it on the table. "I think whoever stole the tankard killed Bitsy and framed Hayden."

Sue sliced a radish into neat circles. "But wasn't the tankard found with Hayden's body?"

"It's fake," said Lucy, opening the cupboard and taking out two plates.

"So the real one is still missing?" Sue's voice was muffled; she'd stuck her head in the refrigerator.

"I just hate myself for thinking this but it must be one of the directors," blurted Lucy. She paused, remembering how flattered she had been to be asked to join the board and how she had agonized over what to wear to her first meeting. "That probably sounds ridiculous — they're all such respectable, hard-working, civic-minded people."

"Oh, I don't know about that, Lucy," said Sue, setting the salad bowl on the table. Hearing the microwave ding, she turned away. "They always seemed like a pretty difficult bunch to me. Bitsy was always complaining about them."

"Miss Tilley certainly didn't like her much," volunteered Lucy.

"Yeah, but she's a little old to be a murderer."

Sue set the casserole on the table and lifted the cover, releasing a wonderful herb-filled fragrance.

"That smells delicious," exclaimed Lucy. "What is it?"

"Cassoulet." Sue was smug.

"Wow. Isn't that hard to make?"

"It is complicated, but now that I have more time, I enjoy cooking things that are a little special."

"It's great," said Lucy, her mouth full of beans and sausage. "Perfect for a cold winter day."

Sue sat down and filled her plate. "If you think about it, none of those directors are exactly paragons of virtue. Take Chuck, for example. He's quite a ladies' man, at least that's what I hear. What if he had some kind of relationship with Bitsy? He wants out, she doesn't. It could get messy. Or Corney? Bitsy knew that her so-called original recipes weren't original at all. They came from cookbooks in the library — at least that's what I've heard."

"Face it — you'd love it to be Corney," said Lucy.

"You're right," agreed Sue, taking a bite of salad. "I hate that column of hers. It just infuriates me, the way she latches onto something and pretends she thought it up in the first place. Like at Christmas, she was writing about Yorkshire pudding as if she invented it." She paused to chew. "Gosh, my grandmother made Yorkshire pudding every year for Christmas, my mother made it, and I make it. We were making it for years before Corney ever heard of it."

"Golly, I guess I touched a nerve here," said Lucy, smiling. She glanced around Sue's stripped-down kitchen, which had evolved during the years she was working so hard at the center. The charming clutter of collectables was gone; it was now an efficient meal-preparation center. "I think you're just jealous."

Sue snorted. "Trust me. There's some sort of deep, dark, disgusting secret there. Nobody is as perfect as Corney pretends to be." She paused, helping herself to seconds of cassoulet. "And she's not the only one. Take Ed, for example. Sid had quite a laugh about that. Said the board would pick the one contractor in town who had a reputation for shoddy construction." Sid was Sue's husband.

"Bill says people are always saying things like that about contractors and it's hardly ever true," said Lucy, loyally defending her husband's chosen trade. "Besides, that new addition speaks for itself. It's beautiful, and it doesn't detract from the original building. That's a hard trick to pull off, believe me."

"Okay," said Sue, amused at her reaction. "But there's still what's-his-name, the college president."

"Gerald?" Lucy asked in surprise.

"Yeah, Gerald. Newly retired from a prestigious job — that can be a very stressful time. All of a sudden he's got a lot of time on his hands. People aren't jumping to answer his every beck and call. It's something to think about."

"Gerald's above reproach," insisted Lucy. "Everybody knows that."

"Those are the worst kind," said Sue, smiling as Zoe came into the room. "Is the movie over already?"

"No." She shook her head sadly. "Bambi's mother died."

"That's a sad part." Sue was sympathetic. "Tell you what. The movie gets better. How about if I come and watch it with you? You can sit in my lap — would you like that?"

Zoe nodded.

"Okay." Sue got up and took the little girl's hand. "We'll let your Mom clean up the lunch dishes, okay?"

"That's not fair!" protested Lucy, pretending to be outraged.

Zoe giggled.

"Don't make too much noise with those dishes," advised Sue. "We want to hear the movie and we don't want to be disturbed. Isn't that right, Zoe?"

"Right!" agreed Zoe, delighted to be telling her mother what to do.

"Well, I guess I'd better get to work then," Lucy said, her voice resigned. Actually, she didn't mind clearing up one bit; she enjoyed the way Zoe and Sue delighted in each other's company.

She scraped the few dishes and gave them a quick rinse, preparing to load them into the dishwasher. Moving automatically, she was wondering how long ago Josiah's Tankard was stolen. Perhaps there were photographs that could establish when the substitution was made.

She opened the dishwasher door and pulled out the wire rack, preparing to load it, but the subtle gleam of a piece of pewter caught her eye. She picked the piece up and held it in front of the window, amazed. It was a perfect copy of Josiah's Tankard, except for the fact that the bird in a bush design had been replaced with the seal of Winchester College.

"Sue!" she yelled, hurrying into the TV room. "Where did you get this?"

Sue looked up from the couch, where she was snuggling with Zoe. "What? That? We've had it forever."

"But where did you get it? When did you get it?"

"Calm down, Lucy. It's not original."

"I know that — it's got the Winchester College seal, for one thing."

"Right. That's it. They made them when the college had its centennial. Sid was doing some work over there, and they gave him one. They were giving them out to everybody."

"What year was that?"

"It was a long time ago — is there something on the tankard?"

Lucy looked closely at the seal on the tankard, and made out the numbers. "It says 1878. That means the centennial was 1978 — just before Bill and I moved here."

"That sounds about right," agreed Sue. "But I don't see why this is so important. I bet most houses in Tinker's Cove have at least one of these things."

"I didn't know that," said Lucy. "Don't you see? This must be how the switch was made. It wouldn't be very hard to get rid of this seal — it's stamped very lightly."

Sue nodded. "It would be easy enough to copy the design from Josiah's Tankard — it was made with a punch. All you'd need is a tenpenny nail and a hammer."

"That's one mystery solved," said Lucy, giving the tankard a little pat.

"Yeah — but I don't think it's going to be much help," said Sue, sitting back down on the couch beside Zoe. "Now you've got a whole town full of suspects."

"You're right." Lucy sat down in the rocking chair and glumly studied the tankard. "You know," she finally said, "the more I find out about this mess, the less I seem to know."

Fifteen

The littlest Billy Goat Gruff was afraid of the troll who dwelled beneath the bridge.

On the way home, Lucy stopped at the Quik-Stop to pick up a gallon of milk. Much to Zoe's disappointment, she left her in the car. If she allowed her in the store, the little girl would insist on choosing a treat and Lucy had no intention of getting involved in the endless negotiations such a purchase required. Besides, she could keep an eye on her through the store window.

In the parking lot, she noticed with disapproval the familiar litter of lottery tickets. Guiltily, she thought of the story she was supposed to be writing for *The Pennysaver*. She had to get it finished; Ted was expecting it in two days, on Friday.

Lucy yanked open the door, intent on dashing over to the dairy case and getting out of the store and back to the car as quickly as possible. Instead, she ran right into Gerald Asquith, trim and distinguished as ever in his camel hair coat.

"I'm sorry!" exclaimed Lucy, growing rather red in the face. "I wasn't watching where I was going."

"Lost in thought, no doubt, thinking about your next writing project," he said, smiling down at her benignly. "No harm done, I assure you."

"I'm glad I ran into you, no pun intended," began Lucy, with an apologetic little smile. "There are a couple of things about the library that I'd like to discuss with you."

Actually, Lucy wanted to find out more about those Winchester College tankards, but didn't want to come right out and say so.

"I can certainly understand that," said Gerald. "You must be wondering why you ever agreed to join the board. I hope you're not thinking of resigning."

"Oh, I wouldn't do that. After all, I just agreed to join the nominating committee. In fact," she continued, improvising, "that's what I'd like to talk about with you."

"Well, why don't we get together for an hour or so?" He withdrew a leather-covered calendar from his breast pocket and opened it. "I'm free tomorrow morning. How would that be?"

"Fine," said Lucy, a little surprised at his promptness. He seemed almost eager to schedule the meeting. "About ten?"

"Ten's fine. Now where shall we meet? Would you like to go someplace for coffee?"

Lucy was flummoxed. She really wanted to get a peek at his house in hopes of learning a little more about him. The way things were going, she wanted to know as much as possible about her fellow board members.

"Oh," she sighed. "I'm trying to lose a few pounds — I'm afraid I gained some weight over the holidays. But I have no will power at all, so I've been avoiding coffee shops." She lowered her eyes as if sharing a shameful secret. "I can't resist the muffins — especially the chocolate chip ones."

He responded just as she hoped he would and chuckled indulgently. "Well, we can't expose you to temptation, can we? How about my house — I have an office there."

"That's fine. I'll see you at ten." agreed Lucy.

As he turned to push open the door, she added, "And remember — no muffins!"

He turned back, gave her the high sign, and left.

Lucy looked past him, checking that Zoe was behaving herself, and was relieved to see the little girl was sitting quietly in her regulation car seat, no doubt hoping that her good behavior would be noticed and rewarded. Finally completing her errand, Lucy joined her a minute later.

"Did you get me something?" Zoe's voice was hopeful.

"I sure did," said Lucy, handing her a foil-covered chocolate heart. "That took longer than I thought it would, but you waited very patiently."

"Thank you," said Zoe, taking the candy and unwrapping it. "Who was the man?"

"Mr. Asquith, from the library."

As Lucy started the car and slipped it into gear, her thoughts returned to the murders. That's how she thought of them — murders. After talking to Ralph and Sue she was more than ever convinced that Hayden had not committed suicide but had been killed, most likely by the same person who killed Bitsy.

Horowitz thought he had the case all wrapped up — Bitsy was murdered by Hayden because she somehow discovered the theft of the tankard. Fearing discovery when Lucy began inquiring about the tankard, Hayden had killed himself. It was all nonsense, of course, just like his allegation that she had been instrumental in Hayden's decision to kill himself. It was so unfair. So frustrating. And worst of all, Horowitz would consider the case closed and the real murderer might never be discovered.

She glanced in the rearview mirror, checking on Zoe. The little girl was chewing contentedly, studying the bright red wrapper. Returning her eyes to the road, Lucy noticed that snowflakes were starting to hit the windshield.

"Uh-oh," she said out loud. "I think it's starting to snow again."

"Yay!" exclaimed Zoe, kicking her heels against the seat.

Lucy couldn't quite share her daughter's enthusiasm. "Haven't you had enough snow yet this winter?" she asked.

"Nope." Zoe shook her head. "I like snow."

"Well, maybe we won't get too much," said Lucy hopefully, thinking aloud. If this turned out to be a big storm, she might not be able to keep her appointment with Gerald. The flakes were falling more thickly now, and she looked at the sky but its whiteness gave her no clue. This could be just a flurry, or a blizzard. She flicked on the aging car radio, hoping for a weather report, but today was not one of its good days and it just buzzed. The uncertainty was driving her nuts, she realized. She wanted to know what to expect.

And that wasn't all, she realized. More than anything she wanted to know who killed Bitsy and Hayden, and why, but if she tried to investigate she ran the risk of angering Horowitz even more. She had no doubt he would file charges against her if he thought she was meddling in the case.

The thought gave her pause. Certainly Horowitz couldn't construe her meeting with Asquith as meddling in the investigation. She was a director, after all, and was responsible for the library. She had every right to talk with the other directors about library business. And there was plenty of business that needed to be settled. Who was going to replace Bitsy? Not to mention Hayden. And what about that security system? The theft of the tankard was even more proof that such a system was needed.

No, she concluded as she turned into her own driveway, there was no way Horowitz could object to her meeting with Asquith. She had plenty of legitimate reasons for the meeting, even if she did nurture the hope that she would discover something that would shed light on the deaths.

Gerald lived in one of the big old sea captain's houses lining Main Street, and Lucy was conscious of the aged condition of her Subaru as she drove between the imposing brick pillars on either side of the circular driveway and parked. The bright sun was merciless; yesterday's dusting of snow had melted, revealing every dent and bit of rust.

The brick steps were wet with the melting snow as Lucy climbed up to the door that was exactly in the center of the Federal-style mansion and tapped the shiny brass knocker. She didn't have time to admire the handsome pinecone wreath before the door opened and she was admitted.

"So nice to see you," said Gerald, taking her hand and drawing her into the center hall. Lucy had a general impression of Oriental rugs, gilt mirrors, and a sweeping stairway before she was installed in Gerald's study. The study, tucked under the stairs, was a cozy, book-lined room featuring a huge, leather-topped desk. She sank into one of the oversized armchairs and wished that she could spend the entire day here, immersed in one of her favorite mystery novels.

"This is a lovely room," she said. "It's a wonderful place to curl up with your favorite book."

"I suppose it is," said Gerald, brushing some crumbs off his desk. "I'm afraid I don't really appreciate it. My wife tends to shoo me in here during the day — she's not used to having me home, you see. I only retired a few months ago."

"I'm awfully glad you could see me," began Lucy. "I've been terribly upset about all this business with the library."

"I really feel that I should apologize — what a terrible time to take up the duties of a director. This is all most unusual, of course. Nothing like this has ever happened before, at least not in the twenty-odd years I've been on the board. First Bitsy, and now Hayden," he said, looking rather bleak. "It's overwhelming."

"I know," said Lucy, staring out the window at the snowy trees. "Do you really think Hayden killed Bitsy?"

"The police think she discovered he'd stolen the tankard," said Gerald.

"You know, something's been bothering me about the tankard," Lucy began slowly.

"I'm no expert on pewter, but I don't think the tankard that was found with Hayden is really Josiah's Tankard."

Gerald's jaw dropped. "You don't?"

"No. I had a chance to look at it quite closely, and it seemed awfully light in weight for a really old piece. And then I learned about the commemorative tankards the college had made, and it seemed a substitution could have been made."

"The college tankards had the Winchester seal . . ." began Gerald.

"I know, but the seal could have been rubbed off easily enough, and replaced with the design. That's why I wanted to ask you about the tankards . . ."

"Have you told anyone about this?" demanded Gerald, cutting her off.

"Only Lieutenant Horowitz."

"Good." Gerald nodded, and once again brushed at the papers on his desk. "I don't think you should tell anyone else. Not until we know for sure."

"Didn't Horowitz tell you about this?" Lucy was puzzled.

Gerald looked at her blankly with his pale blue eyes, and his Adam's apple bobbed. "Maybe he did," he finally decided. "It may have slipped my mind." He attempted a little chuckle. "One of the

217

penalties of old age — I don't seem to re-member things as well as I used to."

Lucy smiled sympathetically. "The other thing that's been bothering me is whether the library has an alarm system. In light of everything that's happened I really think it ought to be a priority."

"I must say that I agree with you. Some of us wanted it included in the new addi-tion, but we were told it was unnecessary."

"Who said that?" Lucy's interest was piqued.

"Well, a few members wanted to keep costs down, anyway, and Ed Bumpus assured us the building would be virtually intruder-proof. Something like that." Gerald gave a little nod and brushed his hand across the desk.

Lucy wasn't sure if it was a nervous habit, or if some sticky crumbs were in-deed clinging to the papers.

"Will the library be opening soon?" in-quired Lucy. "If you need volunteers to staff the desk, or anything else for that matter, I'd be happy to help."

"Thank you, but that won't be necessary. Eunice is a thorough professional. She was one of the college librarians until she re-tired a few months ago and I asked her if she would take over temporarily. Actually, she jumped at the chance."

"That's wonderful," said Lucy enthusiastically. Then an unwelcome thought struck her. "You are sure she'll be safe?"

"Of course. Why not?"

"Well — two people are dead," said Lucy, feeling that she was restating the obvious.

Gerald pursed his lips and drummed the table with his long, slender fingers. He touched the latest issue of *The Pennysaver*, just out that morning. "According to this, the police say the investigation is closed. They're the experts, and they're satisfied. I think it's time to move on."

"You're right," conceded Lucy. "The most important thing we can do right now is to get the library up and running again."

Gerald opened a folder, taking out a sheet of paper. Once again, he brushed it off. "We were planning on dedicating the new addition in a few weeks, but I think we ought to postpone it until all this has died down."

"That's probably best," said Lucy, standing to go. "Thanks for taking the time to meet with me."

"No problem at all," said Gerald, taking her hand in his.

Lucy was shocked. His hand was icy

cold, and his grip was unpleasantly tight.

"Please remember," he said, his eyes meeting hers. His usual smile was gone and his jaw was set in a hard line. "Investigations of this sort are best left to the police. You have a family to think of. If, as you suspect, the murderer is still at large, well, I wouldn't want to see you become the next victim." His lips twitched, almost as if he was attempting a smile but couldn't quite manage it. "Take care."

"I will, I certainly will," said Lucy, stumbling slightly as she left the room.

In the hallway she encountered a tall woman with gray hair, neatly dressed in a blue twin sweater set and a wool tweed skirt.

"You must be Lucy Stone," she said, smiling warmly. "Gerald told me you would be coming. I'm Lucretia Asquith."

"It's nice to meet you," stammered Lucy. "I was just leaving."

"I'll see you to the door, then. I hope you'll come back again soon so we can get to know one another."

"Me, too," said Lucy, hurrying out the door. She knew she was being rude, but she couldn't help it. She had an irrational urge to flee, to get away from that house and Gerald Asquith as fast as she could.

Sixteen

The Snow Queen lived in a beautiful castle made of ice.

Once she was safe in her car, driving over to the Orensteins' to pick up Zoe, Lucy considered her reaction to Gerald's comment. She must have misunderstood his meaning, she decided. He wasn't the sort of man who went around making threats; he had probably just been warning her not to get involved in a dangerous situation. He was probably sincerely worried about her.

Worry, as she well knew, wasn't always entirely rational. And the situation at the library would have to be especially distressing to the older, more conservative board members, like Gerald. Nothing like this had ever happened before. It must seem to Gerald that his formerly sedate and ordered world had suddenly turned topsy-turvy.

What she needed, what they all needed,

she decided as she turned into the Orensteins' driveway, was time to gain a little perspective on the situation.

"You're here already?" exclaimed Juanita, as she opened the door. "I had no idea it was so late."

"No problems, then?"

Juanita waved her hand, dismissing the very idea. "Not with these two — they get on like a house afire. They've been playing in Sadie's room all morning."

"That's terrific," said Lucy. "It's our turn next — maybe Sadie can come over one day next week?"

The fine weather continued to hold as Lucy and Zoe drove home. There wasn't a cloud in the sky and the temperature was a balmy 30 degrees according to the revolving sign in front of the bank. After lunch, she decided, they'd have to get outside for some fresh air. It would do them both good.

Lucy noticed the blinking light on the answering machine when she got the plates out of the cupboard, and listened to her messages while she made tuna sandwiches for herself and Zoe.

"Hey, Lucy, Ted here. I'd like to use your gambling story in next week's paper — let me know when it will be ready, okay?"

Jeez Louise, thought Lucy guiltily. With everything that had happened lately she had forgotten all about the story. The research was all done — she just had to write the darn thing. Maybe she'd have a chance to work on it later this afternoon.

"Lucy, it's me," began the next message and Lucy recognized Sue's voice. "I got a flyer from the Portland Galleria — it's that time of the year again. How about shopping 'til we drop this weekend? Either Saturday or Sunday is fine with me. Give me a call, will ya?"

Lucy smiled. She always enjoyed shopping with Sue, who was an expert at sniffing out bargains. And this was a terrific time to find them, now that the stores were holding their big clearance sales.

She began a mental list as she set the plates on the table and poured two glasses of milk. Bill needed some new long underwear, Elizabeth needed pajamas and hadn't gotten any for Christmas, Toby needed socks. They could use some new towels, and she'd love to have a new dress to wear for her Valentine's Day dinner with Bill at the Greengage Cafe.

"Did you have a nice time at Sadie's this morning?" she asked Zoe.

"Sadie has Diamond-Dazzle Barbie. She

has a crown. And the matching Ken has a shiny silver jacket."

"Wow," said Lucy, who could just imagine the total effect. "They must be . . . beautiful."

"Not Ken," Zoe corrected her. "He's handsome."

"Handsome is as handsome does," recited Lucy. "Does he behave himself?"

"He does whatever Barbie says."

Lucy couldn't help chuckling at this glimpse of Zoe's ordered imaginary universe, in which the newest, most glamorous Barbie was the indisputable queen of all she surveyed.

"Next week when Sadie comes you can play with your new Barbie — what's she called? Extremely Emerald?"

"No, Mommy. She's Emerald Elegance." Having straightened up that little misunderstanding, Zoe slid down from her chair and trotted off to the family room to save Funny Bunny from the evil electronic elves.

Standing at the kitchen sink, Lucy looked out the window at Red Top Hill. Thanks to the strong sunlight and the mild temperature, a few bare patches of asphalt were beginning to appear on the icy road. The steep hill just beyond the driveway was still covered with snow, however. They were the last house on the road and hardly anyone drove past this time of year; even the school bus turned around rather than following the hilly twists and turns that led past Blueberry Pond and eventually back to town.

For a moment, as she regarded the snowy hill, Lucy was a little girl again, tucked safely between her father's arms as he guided their speeding six-foot Flexible Flyer past the snow-mounded cars lining the still city street and took her swooping down Reservoir Road. She screamed all the way, she remembered, and he thought she had been frightened. No, she told him, she was screaming because it was so much fun.

Shutting the dishwasher door, Lucy decided that Funny Bunny would be there tomorrow and every other day, but the conditions on Red Top Hill Road were rarely this ideal for sliding.

"Come on, Zoe," she called. "We're going to see just how fast we can get my old sled to go."

The paint had worn off the old Flexible Flyer years ago, and the rope was frayed, but the runners were still bright silver thanks to the coating of oil Lucy rubbed on them every time she put the sled away.

"Won't it be dangerous in the road, Mommy?" asked Zoe.

"I don't think so," said Lucy, standing at the top of the hill and surveying the situation. As she thought, yesterday's light snowfall on top of the tightly packed snow beneath it would provide an ideal sliding surface. The fresh snow was just beginning to soften up and it would give them just the slippery surface they needed for maximum speed. "Nobody's been along here all day, and even if somebody comes they'll have to drive pretty slowly," said Lucy. "We'll have plenty of time to see them."

"Okay," said Zoe, with the solemnity of an Olympic contender. "I'm ready."

"Me, too," said Lucy, settling herself on the sled and tucking Zoe between her legs. Unlike her father, she preferred to go down feet first. She pushed off with her arms, and the sled inched along, gradually picking up speed until they were flying down the hill so fast that the snow-covered trees seemed to whizz by them. At the bottom, Lucy pushed the steering bar with her feet, hoping to brake into a neat circle. Instead, they rolled off into the snow, shrieking and laughing.

Lucy heard her joints creak as she got back on her feet and knew that her muscles would undoubtedly be sore the next day. That's what they invented ibuprofen for, she thought, as she brushed the snow off her face.

"Again?" she asked Zoe.

"Yes!" screamed the little girl, her eyes sparkling above apple-red cheeks. She took off, running up the hill, while Lucy followed more slowly, towing the sled.

An hour or so later, Lucy and Zoe were extracting themselves from some scratchy blueberry bushes when they heard the familiar groan of the gears on the school bus as it prepared to climb the other side of the hill. They ran up to meet it, waving at Moe, the bus driver.

"Mother, don't tell me you've been sliding," said Elizabeth, twisting her lips into a scowl and rolling her black eyeliner-lined eyes. "Thank goodness none of my friends are still on the bus."

"What friends?" Toby asked predictably. "You don't have any friends."

"Do, too."

"Who? Lard-face Lance?" teased her older brother, referring to Elizabeth's on-again, off-again boyfriend.

"You're disgusting," said Elizabeth, turning her back and trudging off toward the house.

"Come on, Toby," begged Sara. "Let's go sliding, too. It looks like fun."

"It is fun," said Zoe. "Lots of fun."

Toby cast an expert eye at the hill. "You know, if we made a little bank of snow at the bottom, we wouldn't go into the bushes."

"That's a good idea," said Lucy, wondering why she hadn't thought of it herself. "I'll get the shovel and start while you get out the sleds and stuff."

Soon Toby and Sara were spinning down the hill in snow saucers, and eventually even Elizabeth appeared, trying out the snowboard she got for Christmas.

Realizing that she was soaked to the skin, Lucy decided to go inside to warm up. Zoe wasn't ready to come in yet, and as Lucy climbed wearily up the hill one last time she smiled to see her littlest one whirling past on a saucer, safe in her big brother's arms.

Back inside the warm kitchen, she tugged off her snow-encrusted hat and mittens and laid them on top of the radiator. Then her boots went in the tray by the door; she unzipped and peeled off her snowsuit, hanging it up in the pantry, next to the water heater. In the powder room, she brushed out her damp hair, hardly recognizing herself in the mirror. With her hat hair and red cheeks, she looked, she realized with a shock, just like the aging photographs of that little girl who went sledding with her father so many years ago.

She put a big pot of hot chocolate on the stove and opened the door to call the kids. Hearing the unfamiliar sound of an engine — a souped-up one at that — she stuffed her feet back into her boots and went out to investigate, drawing her sweater tightly across her chest.

As she ran down the driveway she heard the engine coming closer; it sounded to her like one of those pick-up trucks with oversized tires. It seemed to be coming from the direction of the pond, along the part of the road that wound through the woods.

She waved at her kids and called to them, but they weren't paying any attention. They didn't seem to be aware of the approaching truck. Toby was seating himself in one of the saucers and Zoe, she saw, was jumping in his lap. He had just pushed off with his arms, and began sailing down the hill, when the truck appeared on the other side, at the bottom of the hill.

Horrified, Lucy saw that it was going way too fast; the driver was probably hoping to build up enough speed to make it up the hill. Sara, standing at the crest, spotted the truck and began waving her arms, trying to warn the driver to slow down. Either he didn't see her, or decided to ignore her and sped up the hill right past her, directly toward the saucer.

Lucy covered her mouth with her hand and held her breath; there was nothing she could do but pray. Toby must have seen the truck by now, and realized the danger he and Zoe were in, but the saucer was impossible to steer. Once started down the hill, there was no way he could change its direction.

It was up to the driver of the truck to do something. "Stop! Stop!" she screamed, knowing there was no possibility that he could hear her. He must see the saucer, though. Why wasn't he stopping?

If only Toby could push the saucer out of the truck's path — but it was spinning toward it. It was only feet from the huge black tires of the truck, she realized, and tears sprang to her eyes. A horrible sound came from her throat, a high-pitched, keening scream.

Then, miraculously, she saw the saucer

tip and curve away from the truck, spilling Toby and Zoe into the snow on the side of the road.

Never stopping, the truck hurtled past her, a roaring blur of black and chrome. Furious, she spun around and tried to make out the license plate, but it was covered with crusted ice.

Clenching her fists, she pounded them once against her thighs, then turned to the kids. They were fine, stamping their feet and shaking the snow out of their hats.

"Come on in," Lucy called to them in a shaky voice. "I've made some hot cocoa."

She stood there in the cold and growing dimness, watching as they plodded up the hill, towing their sleds and saucers. She wasn't chilled at all; she was furious. How could the driver of that truck have been so irresponsible? Could it be possible that he didn't see them?

Lucy didn't think so. There had been plenty of light and the kids were dressed in bright clothes; they were out in the open on the snowy hill. They were highly visible. In fact, she realized with a shock, it had almost seemed as if the driver had been driving directly toward them. But that was absurd, she thought. Nobody would do a thing like that.

Trudging back to the house, Lucy resolved to ask Barney if any of the local youths had a particularly reckless reputation, and a fancy truck to go with it. He would probably know who the driver was; he might even have a word with him.

Then again, perhaps she shouldn't report it. She wouldn't like to get some kid in trouble over some cold-weather high jinks.

That was ridiculous, she decided, marching along the driveway. She had her family to think of. She stopped dead in her tracks. Where had she heard that lately? From Gerald Asquith?

Oh, no. She brushed the thought away. This was an accident. A near miss by some kid with more horsepower than sense. There was no way Gerald could have had anything to do with it. No way at all.

Seventeen

*Every time he told a lie, Pinocchio's
nose grew a little longer.*

When the alarm went off the next morning,
Lucy confused it with the scream of an ambulance. She had a brief, terrifying image of
a black-and-chrome truck hurtling through
the snow and crashing into the Subaru. But
when she opened her eyes, she was safe in
bed beside Bill.

She rolled over, reaching for the alarm
clock, and moaned in pain. She was getting
a bit old for sledding, she decided. Everything hurt: arms, back, and most painful of
all, her thighs.

"I'm not as young as I used to be," she
moaned, cautiously pulling herself to a sitting position.

"Why don't you lie in for a bit," suggested Bill. "I'll bring you breakfast in
bed."

"Oh, no," said Lucy. "I don't dare. If I

lie down, I might never get back up." She sighed, and groped for her slippers with her feet. "There *is* one thing you could do for me."

"Sure. What is it?"

"Put my slippers on for me," she asked plaintively.

After the kids had left for school, Lucy sat at the kitchen table, nursing a cup of coffee. She had filled Bill's lunchbox and was waiting to say good-bye to him. But when he appeared, reaching over her shoulder for the box, she held his arm.

"Do you know anybody who has a black-and-chrome pick-up?" she asked.

"Probably. Why do you want to know?"

"One came tearing up the road yesterday, when the kids were sledding. It was a close call. We were lucky."

Bill sat down, scratching his bearded chin. "Ed's got one like that, I think."

"That's right. I saw it at the food pantry. It could've been that truck."

"He's a pretty careful driver, though," said Bill, shaking his head. "Doesn't sound like him."

"Maybe someone who works for him?"

"If I see him, I'll ask him," said Bill, standing up. He stroked her cheek with his hand. "If the kids want to slide, have 'em stay in the yard, okay?"

If confession is good for the soul, Lucy figured her soul must be in tiptop shape this morning. She thought she'd handled telling Bill about the kids' near miss pretty well. She'd told him just as he was getting ready to leave the house, his mind already on the day ahead. And by asking him about the truck, she'd neatly positioned him as her helper, not her critic.

A psychological masterpiece, she decided, having left Zoe at Kiddie Kollege and heading over to *The Pennysaver* office. If only she could manage Ted as well.

The little bell on the door tinkled as she pulled it open, causing Ted to look up from his desk.

"Hi, Lucy. Have you got the story?"

"No."

"No?"

"Please don't yell. I'm in a lot of pain."

"What happened?"

"I was in kind of an accident yesterday. I was sledding with the kids and a big truck . . ."

"Are you all right?" Ted hopped to his feet and began clearing files off a chair. "Sit down."

"Thanks," said Lucy, allowing herself to groan as she lowered herself onto the seat. "I'm just sore all over."

"What about the kids?"

"They're fine. It was just a near miss, but I was too upset to work on the story."

"Take all the time you need," he said, magnanimously. "Actually, I have some features left over from this week that I didn't use. What a week — murder, suicide, theft all tied up in a neat little bundle. It doesn't get much better than this." He paused and shook his head regretfully. "If only they'd been lovers."

"Who? Bitsy and Hayden?" Lucy raised an eyebrow. "Not much chance of that."

"I know, I know," Ted hastened to say. "I was only saying that it would have been a nice touch."

"Well, it would have made the whole thing more understandable," admitted Lucy. "I can't for the life of me think what would possess Hayden to do these things."

"Horowitz is pretty definite about it — he was quite chatty, in fact. Pretty unusual for the great stone face."

"He thinks he's got a nice, tidy case, all tied up with a bow," fumed Lucy. "He isn't going to go looking for loose ends, is he? He wants the case closed. He didn't know

Hayden — he doesn't know how ridiculous this whole thing is."

"Oh, ho," mused Ted. "So you don't agree with the official solution?"

"Not by a long shot," admitted Lucy. "Hey, thanks for being so nice about the story. I absolutely, positively promise I'll have it for you next week."

"I've heard that before," said Ted, looking doubtful.

It was barely ten when Lucy left *The Pennysaver* office, walking carefully down Main Street to her car. The sidewalk was clear but there were icy patches and the last thing she wanted to do was fall. The way she felt, she'd never get up again. The ibuprofen she'd taken earlier was helping, but her arms and legs still ached.

In the car, Lucy considered her options. Zoe wouldn't be out of Kiddie Kollege until twelve. She could spend that time in a hot tub; the only problem was she didn't know anybody who had one. Besides, she wouldn't be able to relax — not even in a hot tub — until she sorted out her emotions, still unsettled from yesterday's near tragedy. She couldn't shake the feeling that Gerald was somehow involved, ridiculous as that seemed. Nevertheless, he had no sooner given her a clear warning to mind her own business than the frightening incident with the truck had occurred. Besides, she had definitely gotten the sense that Gerald was hiding something, but how could she find out what it was?

She put the key in the ignition and adjusted the rear view mirror, catching sight of the gift she had wrapped for Miss Tilley. With everything that had been happening, she had forgotten all about it. No time like the present, she decided, slipping the Subaru into drive and turning up the heater.

Rachel greeted her warmly when she opened the door.

"Lucy! What a nice surprise! Come on in out of the cold — I've got the kettle on."

"That sounds great," said Lucy, with chattering teeth. "Why is it that the car heater doesn't kick in until you're wherever it is that you're going?"

"Just one of those things, I guess," said Rachel, taking her coat. "Sit down by the fire."

Miss Tilley was seated in her usual rocking chair on one side of the fireplace, a brightly colored, crocheted afghan covering her legs.

"Don't you make a cozy picture," began Lucy, holding out the present. "This is for you. To let you know how badly I felt about quarreling with you last week."

"There's no need for an apology," said Miss Tilley, as she took the present. Her eyes were bright with amusement. "I'm a quarrelsome old biddy. Such behavior shouldn't be rewarded, should it, Rachel?"

"Absolutely not," said Rachel, as she carried in the tea tray. "You'll undo all my efforts to civilize this old witch."

"I could take it back . . ." began Lucy.

"Never mind." Miss Tilley flapped her hand, shooing her away. "Since you've gone to all this trouble I don't want to disappoint you."

"All right, then," said Lucy, taking a cup and cautiously seating herself in the comfortable armchair on the other side of the fireplace. "I'll let you keep it. I hope you like it."

Miss Tilley's fingers trembled as she unwrapped the present, another sign of her increasing debility. Lucy didn't watch her struggle, but studied the bright flames dancing in the fireplace and concentrated on relaxing her painful, tensed muscles.

"This is lovely! Thank you," exclaimed Miss Tilley.

Lucy looked up and smiled at her. "I thought it might remind you of Josiah's Tankard."

"It does — it's very similar, isn't it?" She ran her fingers over the smooth surface and wrapped them around the handle. "You really didn't need to do this, you know."

"I know," Lucy said, smiling. "I wanted to."

"Where shall we put it?" asked Rachel. "On the mantel?"

Before Lucy could suggest the tavern table, Miss Tilley pointed to it. "Over there, I think. In the light from the window."

Rachel carried the tankard across the room and placed it on the little round, pumpkin-colored table. It seemed to sit happily there, quietly glowing, as if it had found a home.

"Perfect," said Rachel, and they all nodded in agreement, admiring the effect. "Well, it's back to the kitchen for me — I've got to keep an eye on my pudding or it will burn."

Lucy took a sip of tea, but spluttered when Miss Tilley abruptly posed a question.

"Have you got to the bottom of this

business at the library yet?" the old woman asked.

"Not quite," admitted Lucy. "But Horowitz thinks he's got the whole thing wrapped up."

"That's ridiculous. Hayden wouldn't have hurt a fly." Miss Tilley's tone was definite.

"You know," began Lucy, determined to confess yet another sin, "when I decided to get you a tankard I asked Corney and Hayden for some advice about pewter. Horowitz said Hayden may have misunderstood my interest — he said it might be my fault that he killed himself."

"That's the most ridiculous thing I've ever heard."

"This is just a theory," began Lucy, "but what if Josiah's Tankard isn't genuine? What if Hayden had switched it? That would be quite a motive for suicide."

"I've had my doubts for a while," admitted Miss Tilley, surprising Lucy with her complacency. "I didn't want to alarm the board unnecessarily, but I was going to suggest having it appraised by an expert. Something about it isn't quite right — but I don't for one minute think Hayden made the switch."

"When did you first notice it?"

"When we had it out the last time — it seemed lighter than I expected."

"When was it last authenticated?" asked Lucy. "Is there documentation of any kind?"

"There is, and I tried to check it, but the file was missing. I meant to pursue it, but I came down with the flu and I never got around to it. Gerald probably knows where it is."

"Of course," said Lucy, leaning forward and reaching for the teapot. "More for you?"

Miss Tilley shook her head, and Lucy refilled her own cup. Settling back in her chair, she decided to ask Miss Tilley about her old friend. "How is Gerald these days? He seems to be managing so well as president of the board, but all this must be taking a toll on him."

"Oh, Gerald's used to managing crises — he used to be president of Winchester College, you know. He faced down mobs of protesting students in the sixties — he'd only been on the job a couple of weeks when they staged a huge demonstration. And since then it's been one thing after another. Why, just before he retired the college trustees voted to ban alcohol on campus — poor Gerald had to tell the fraternities!" Miss Tilley cackled merrily. "I guess if he could handle that, he could handle anything."

"He must have been glad to retire," ventured Lucy.

"I don't know about that." Miss Tilley was suddenly solemn. "I hated having to retire, and I suspect Gerald felt the same way. It's hard to give up something you love."

"I'm sure it is." Lucy's voice was soft. "But he seems quite busy. I suppose he's on a number of boards. He must have investments to manage. And then there's golf and traveling. I've heard retirees say that they're busier in retirement than they were when they worked."

"I don't think that's quite the case with Gerald." Miss Tilley folded her hands in her lap and looked out the window at the bird feeder where a blue jay had suddenly alighted, scattering the chickadees and titmice that had been gathered there. "Blue jays are such bullies," she said. "I wouldn't allow it, if they weren't so handsome."

"Lunch is almost ready," said Rachel, appearing in the doorway. "Will you stay, Lucy?"

"No, thanks. I have to pick up Zoe. I didn't realize it was so late."

"Well, come back anytime," said Rachel, pulling Lucy's coat out of the hall closet. "You're always welcome."

"Especially when you bring presents," added Miss Tilley, nodding toward the tankard.

"Honestly, she's no better than a five-year-old," clucked Rachel.

"I'm no better than I ought to be — and neither are you!" shot back the old woman.

"I'm afraid that none of us are," said Lucy, giving a little wave as she went out the door. "And some of us are a good deal worse," she muttered as she climbed into the car. She started the engine, shifted to drive, and carefully checked for traffic before pulling away from the curb. It wasn't something she'd care to admit, even to herself, but she didn't want to risk another encounter with that black-and-chrome truck.

Eighteen

The Fairy Godmother waved her magic wand and Cinderella's rags became a beautiful ball gown.

Saturday morning found Lucy sitting at the kitchen table, enjoying a second cup of coffee and reading the morning paper while she waited for Sue to pick her up. The house was unusually quiet; Bill had taken the younger kids ice skating on Blueberry Pond, and Toby and Elizabeth were still sleeping.

Hearing Sue's horn, Lucy struggled painfully into her coat, grabbed her gloves and bag, and hobbled out to Sue's brand-new car, an enormous sport utility vehicle guaranteed to be virtually unstoppable.

"What's the matter with you?" asked Sue, as Lucy hauled herself up into the passenger side seat. Her muscles were still sore and she couldn't help groaning as she strapped the seatbelt on.

"I'm stiff and sore from sledding with the kids."

"About time you acted your age," teased Sue, who avoided exercise like the plague. "Serves you right. You should have been sipping tea and nibbling scones safe indoors."

"You're probably right," agreed Lucy. "Let's have lunch someplace nice, okay? No fast food."

"Fine by me," said Sue, carefully maneuvering the enormous four-wheel drive vehicle, complete with a rhino guard, out of the driveway.

"I always feel so safe in your car," said Lucy, observing the mounds of snow that lined the road. "It's good to know that if a wild rhino should decide to charge, we're ready."

"You never know," said Sue. "It's good to be prepared. Say, are you going to Hayden's funeral tomorrow? I heard Ralph hired Corney to do the food. No expense spared."

"I guess I should — being on the board and all."

"Don't give me that — you wouldn't miss it for the world." Funerals were major social events in Tinker's Cove, and were discussed for months afterward.

"I wonder what she'll serve?"

"Whatever it is, you can be sure she stole the recipe from somebody," said Sue.

"Are there rules about that? Corney told me that as long as you add something new to a recipe you can claim it as your own."

"Hmmph," snorted Sue. "I think it takes more than a pinch of salt or a dusting of parsley to create a new recipe, and I'm not the only one. Laura Winkle — she works over in the courthouse, you know — told me that somebody was suing Corney for copyright infringement. I don't remember who, but I do know they were planning on calling poor Bitsy as a witness. Of course, they can't do that now. Maybe they'll settle out of court."

"Would something like that be a motive for murder?" Lucy was skeptical.

"Laura said they were asking for half a million in damages."

"Gee, sounds like a motive to me," mused Lucy. "Do you think Corney knows how to use a gun?"

"Sure." Sue chuckled. "Keep watching her column. 'A quick and easy way to clean your chimney'."

Lucy laughed. " 'Exterminating pests — easier than you thought'."

"Make your own colander."

"Painless pumpkin carving."

"Don't remind me," moaned Sue. Her attempt to follow Corney's directions for a Victorian lace Halloween pumpkin had resulted in a badly nicked finger that became infected and required a trip to the emergency room and an expensive course of antibiotics. "It isn't that I don't think Corney is capable of murder, I just think she would prefer a less direct method."

"Like tossing a few toxic mushrooms into the coq au vin?"

"Exactly."

"But even if she had a motive to kill Bitsy, why did she have to kill Hayden?" asked Lucy, twisting a lock of hair around her finger.

"He could have figured out that she killed Bitsy," speculated Sue. "And don't forget, he knew a lot about cooking, too. Maybe he knew what a phony she really is."

"Oh, my," said Lucy. "Do you think all this animosity might be because you're jealous of Corney?"

"Absolutely not," insisted Sue. "Why would I be jealous of her?"

Lucy didn't answer; she was looking out the window at the dirty wall of snow that lined the highway. The sky was a dark slate gray and a few flakes were beginning to fall. "I wish winter would end," she said.

"Me, too," sighed Sue.

Once they were inside the Galleria, Portland's newest and most elegant mall complete with potted palm trees and fountains, they forgot all about the weather outside. They lingered over lunch in the Parrot's Perch, enjoying glasses of white wine with their salads. Then they ventured into the stores, where the clearance sales were in full swing. Lucy made quick work of her list, and was seriously considering splurging on a designer dress.

"It's a Diane Fish dress — trust me, you can't go wrong," urged Sue.

"But it's ninety dollars."

"A steal. See the tag. It was over three hundred."

"I could wear it to the funeral," rationalized Lucy, who really wanted it for her Valentine's Day dinner with Bill.

"It's a classic. You can wear it anywhere. Trust me. You'll hate yourself if you don't get it."

"You think it's that good a deal?"

Sue rolled her eyes. "Just look at it. The buttons are all different. Handmade, I bet. And it has pockets. Removable shoulder pads. You don't find these features in cheap dresses."

"I know." Lucy sighed. "It's just that I haven't even paid all the Christmas bills yet."

"Hey — I just remembered. I got a coupon in the mail. It's like a scratch ticket — it said you can save up to seventy-five percent on sale prices."

"Really?"

"Probably not," said Sue, rummaging in her purse. "But you could save something. Ah-ha! Here it is!"

"It doesn't say how much you save," said Lucy.

"Right. You take it to the salesclerk and scratch the little gray circle. She'll take off whatever percent is printed under it."

"What if it's only ten percent?"

Sue sighed. "Tell her you changed your mind."

"And you don't want this ticket?"

"No!" exclaimed Sue. "I really want you to get this nice new dress that is an absolutely terrific bargain and would look great on you and you're really beginning to get on my nerves!"

"Okay. Okay," said Lucy, taking the ticket. "But I'm warning you — I'm not going to get it unless it's at least fifty percent off."

"Whatever," said Sue, waving her arm and dramatically collapsing into a chair outside the fitting rooms.

Lucy approached the cash register, which was staffed by a tired-looking woman with swollen ankles. "Cash or charge?"

"Charge," said Lucy, producing her card. As if it were an afterthought, she added, "Oh, I have this coupon."

"Here you go," said the clerk, handing her a shiny new penny. "Just scratch off the gray circle."

Lucy worked at the circle, brushing away the rubbery crumbs produced by the scratching. "Wow!" she exclaimed. "It says seventy-five."

"Good for you," said the clerk. "Most of them are for ten or twenty percent. That brings your total to twenty-two fifty."

"That's great!" enthused Lucy. "That's a three-hundred-dollar dress."

"It pays to shop at Waldrons'," said the tired salesclerk, repeating the store's slogan.

"I guess it does," nodded Lucy. She took her bag and went over to Sue, who was leaning back in the chair with her eyes closed, a mountain of packages piled on her lap.

"How'd you do?" she asked, without opening her eyes.

"Seventy-five."

"Seventy-five dollars? Not bad."

"No — seventy-five percent off."

Sue's eyes popped open. "You're kidding."

"Nope."

"Damn."

"Something the matter?"

"If I'd known, I would have kept it for myself," she muttered. "I'm ready for a break — how about a cappuccino?"

That night, after doling out her purchases to the kids, Lucy went upstairs to try on the new dress. As she took it out of the bag she noticed that some of the scratch ticket crumbles were stuck to the tissue paper. Thoughtfully, she picked them up and with her thumb rolled them against her fingers. They reminded her of something, but she couldn't quite remember what. Brushing off her hands, she lifted the dress and slipped it over her head. She was standing in front of the mirror when Bill appeared behind her.

"Zip me up?" she asked.

"Okay," he said, with a twinkle in his

eye. "If I can unzip you later."

"Deal," said Lucy, turning to face him and wrapping her arms around his neck.

Nineteen

The Queen was furious and threw the Magic Mirror against the wall.

"God, I hate funerals," said Bill, giving his tie a tug. He was seated beside Lucy in the hushed, flower-scented sanctuary of St. Christopher's Episcopal Church.

Funeral regulars who had come to the earlier visiting hours to gape at Hayden's embalmed body — "Doesn't he look wonderful?" — were certainly disappointed. Not only was there no open casket, there was no casket at all since Hayden had been cremated. Ralph had chosen to have a memorial service, and a very simple one at that. No eulogies. No sharing of personal remembrances of the departed. Just beautiful music played by a string quartet and a simple reading from the *Book of Common Prayer.*

Looking around the church, Lucy noticed that it was filled with unfamiliar faces. This was not the usual Tinker's Cove crowd; these folks were wearing city clothes and their hair, both the men's and the women's, had been styled by hair-dressers with more skill than Moe the Barber or the girls at Dot's Beauty Spot. These people were buffed and massaged, stylish and polished, and Lucy was glad she was wearing her new dress.

"I wish they'd get started," complained Bill.

"It *has* started," whispered Lucy. "It's just music."

"Hunh," grunted Bill. "Who are all these people?"

"Antiques dealers, interior designers, Hayden's clients . . . he was very big in the antiques world."

"Oh," said Bill, unimpressed. In a few minutes his breathing grew regular and Lucy knew he had fallen asleep. He gave a little snort and she elbowed him, afraid he would start snoring. His eyes opened for a second, then closed, and he was off in dreamland once again.

Lucy relaxed against the back of the pew, allowing her mind to drift with the music. There in the front pew she caught a glimpse of Ralph, somber in his black suit. She remembered having coffee with them, and how much they enjoyed each other. Tears began welling in her eyes and she tried to fight them back. Think about something else, don't think about Hayden. Just listen to the music, she told herself, following the soaring notes of a violin solo.

Her eyes roamed around the church and lit on the cross that stood on the altar. It was unusually simple for an Episcopalian church, she thought, realizing it was made of pewter instead of silver. It had to be the tankard, she thought, chewing on her lip. Two people associated with the library were dead, and the tankard was a fake — there had to be a connection. What had Miss Tilley told her? That Gerald had all the documents authenticating the tankard?

What she wanted, she decided, was to take a look at those papers. What she didn't want, however, was another encounter with Gerald. The man gave her the willies.

She looked around the church and spotted him sitting by a stained glass window with Lucretia beside him. She was being ridiculous, she thought, studying his profile. With his gray hair, his strong, angular nose, and his firm jaw, he was still a handsome man — the very image of New England respectability.

Her lips twitched when she remembered Miss Tilley telling her that most of the highly revered New England sea captains hadn't been above smuggling or blockade running, if the profits were high enough. "Pirates, all of them," she'd proclaimed.

There was something of the pirate about Gerald, realized Lucy. He took pains to disguise it, she thought, but she had sensed a tension about him, a certain wariness, that indicated hidden depths. Gerald wasn't entirely respectable.

She would call him tomorrow, she decided, and if he suggested a meeting she would insist that she was too busy. She would tell him to return the documents to Miss Tilley; a good idea, she realized, because it would give her request extra weight.

That settled, Lucy bowed her head and sent up a silent prayer that Ralph would find comfort. The music stopped and the priest stepped up to the lectern. "Please join me in saying the words of Jesus Christ: Our father, who art in heaven . . ."

After the service, Lucy and Bill followed the crowd to the reception in the parish hall. They stood in line and shook hands with Ralph, who looked leaner and handsomer than ever in his dark suit. He, in turn, introduced them to Hayden's parents. Mrs. Northcross was a tiny woman with dyed red hair, dressed in a black suit with a fussy, ruffled white blouse underneath the jacket. Mr. Northcross towered over her, with a bald head and a fringe of white hair. They seemed confused and bewildered by this reversal of the natural order; they hadn't expected to outlive their son.

Lucy took their hands and murmured how sorry she was, wishing she could think of something truly comforting to say. Funerals always made her feel depressed and inadequate.

Bill pressed his hand against her back and steered her toward the buffet set up along the wall on the opposite side of the room. Corney had really outdone herself, thought Lucy, filling her plate with tiny salmon sandwiches, cheese puffs, and stuffed mushrooms.

"Watching our weight, are we?" asked Sue, appearing beside her.

"I didn't have any lunch," lied Lucy.

"Liar," said Sue. "The dress looks nice."

"Thanks." Lucy took a bite of stuffed mushroom. "When I die I want something like this. Simple and tasteful."

"And no expense spared."

"Absolutely. After all, you can't take it with you," agreed Lucy, watching as Corney refreshed a tray of crudités. "Are you sure about that lawsuit?"

"Not really, it was just something I heard," admitted Sue, sipping a glass of white wine.

"I suppose I could check at the courthouse."

"I suppose you could," said Sue, smiling and nodding to someone across the room. "Don't look now, but your friend the lieutenant is here."

"He is? Where?" demanded Lucy, scanning the crowded room.

"He's staring right at you," said Sue. "From behind the coffee urn."

"Oh, I see him. But he's not looking at me." As Lucy watched, the detective took something out of his pocket and studied it, then carefully replaced it. "I wonder what he's doing here. After all, the case is supposed to be closed."

"Well," said Sue, nibbling on a piece of celery, "I don't think he's here for the food. He's not eating anything."

"That's Horowitz for you," said Lucy. "That man doesn't know how to have a good time." She put down her plate on a nearby table. "Well, that was delicious but now it's time to circulate."

She made her way across the crowded room to a spot between the windows where Bill was talking with Ed Bumpus.

"I should have known I'd find you talking construction," said Lucy, taking Bill's arm. "It's nice to see you, Ed."

"Hayden got quite a turnout," said Ed, popping a tiny piece of toast topped with beef tartare into his mouth. "Even if some of these folks walk a little lightly in their shoes, if you get my drift." He chewed thoughtfully. "I can tell you — I was sure glad to see Bill here. There's no question Bill's a straight-up kind of guy. Not like these here . . . well, y'know what I mean."

"That's Bill," said Lucy brightly. "He's hard-working, reliable, trustworthy. You can count on him."

"I know — and that's why I had him look over the figures for the library addition." He gave Bill a hearty slap on the back. "It means a lot to me to know that if anything is ever questioned I can say, 'Bill Stone said it was all okeydokey.' "

"Has anybody been questioning the figures?" Lucy asked curiously.

"Only Chuck," said Ed, indicating the lawyer, who was chatting with Mrs. Asquith.

"That guy gives me a pain in the ass."

"What do you expect? He's a lawyer," said Bill, shrugging philosophically.

"He's probably being extra careful, because of everything that's happened," speculated Lucy.

"I don't care what he is," said Ed, an angry tone creeping into his voice. "He's got no reason to question me. I've got a reputation in this town, y'know."

That's right, Lucy thought to herself, and it's not all that good, from what I've heard. "Hey, Ed," she began. "You know that nice truck of yours? It wasn't out our way lately, on Red Top Road, was it?"

"Not that I know of," said Ed, a note of caution in his voice. "Why?"

"One just like it came tearing down the road the other day when my kids were sledding. It gave me a real scare."

Ed popped a huge stuffed mushroom in his mouth and chewed noisily. "Dunno nuffin' 'bout it," he said, wiping his greasy fingers on his trousers.

"All's well that ends well, I guess."

"That's right," said Bill. "The kids shouldn't have been in the road, anyway."

"Say, Bill," began Ed, turning his back on her, "whaddya think of these new steel two-by-fours?"

No longer included in the conversation, Lucy headed for the coffee table in search of Horowitz, but he was nowhere to be seen. She took a cup and sipped at it, peering over the rim, and spotted the detective striding purposefully across the crowded room. As Lucy watched, he took Gerald by the elbow and led him through the doorway.

Lucy followed them into the hallway, where a uniformed policeman was waiting. She watched, astonished, as Gerald was quickly handcuffed and marched outside to a cruiser which spun off rapidly down the street.

Blinking her eyes in disbelief, Lucy looked around the room to see if anyone else had noticed. But the whole thing had happened so quickly that no one seemed to have seen a thing. No one, that is, except for Lucretia Asquith. Tall and trim as ever, she was pale with shock.

Lucy took her arm and led her out of the crowded room and into an empty office.

"What happened?" she asked Lucy, nervously rubbing her hands together.

"Gerald was arrested," said Lucy, filling a paper cup from the water cooler in the corner and handing it to her. "Do you have any idea why?"

Mrs. Asquith took a sip of water and shook her head.

Lucy noticed a sprinkling of dandruff on the shoulders of her black suit. Suddenly, she remembered the way Gerald had brushed at the papers on his desk.

"He gambled, didn't he?" asked Lucy, thinking of the little gray crumbles she had scratched off the coupon in the store the day before. The words were out before she knew it.

Mrs. Asquith sagged in the chair and Lucy grabbed for the cup before it spilled. She lifted it to the older woman's lips, holding it so Lucretia could take a sip.

"We're going to lose everything," she whispered.

"Everything?" Lucy was stunned. The Asquiths were worth a pretty penny.

"The house is in foreclosure."

"Oh, my God."

Mrs. Asquith nodded grimly. "He always gambled a little bit, but never enough to matter. Then he retired. He couldn't control it anymore. The lottery, scratch tickets, even casinos."

Lucy chewed her lip. "But gambling's not illegal," she said. "Why did they arrest him?"

Mrs. Asquith studied her hands in her lap.

"Did he steal?" asked Lucy.

Mrs. Asquith suddenly jerked back in her chair, and her hands flew to her head. She yanked at her hair and then dissolved into tears.

"There, there," said Lucy, trying to calm her. She was terrified Mrs. Asquith was becoming hysterical.

"I hate him!" she hissed, pounding her hand on the desk. "I hate him for doing this to me."

"Just hang on," said Lucy, patting Mrs. Asquith's shoulder and handing her a tissue. She looked nervously toward the door. "I don't think anybody saw but us. Wait here and I'll get my husband. We'll drive you home."

A shudder ran through the older woman's body, and she began twisting and shredding the paper hankie.

Lucy left, closing the door, and hurried down the hall to the parish room. The crowd had thinned, she noticed. She caught Bill's eye and he came across the room to her.

"I've been looking for you — where've you been?" he asked.

"You won't believe it," she whispered. "Horowitz arrested Gerald Asquith, just a minute ago. I've got a hysterical Mrs. Asquith in the church office. Can you help me get her home?"

"I'll drive her car — you follow, okay?"

"Thanks." Lucy was truly grateful; she could always count on Bill.

She surveyed the coat rack and decided a black cashmere with a fur collar and a light dusting of dandruff was probably Mrs. Asquith's. She pulled it off the hanger and led Bill to the office. There, he gently drew Mrs. Asquith to her feet and Lucy draped the coat over her shoulders. Then, Mrs. Asquith's keys in his hand, he hurried off to bring the car around. Lucy slipped into her coat and waited with Lucretia in the hallway until he pulled up in a black Lincoln town car.

He opened the door on the passenger side and waited as Lucy escorted the older woman down the icy pathway and helped her into the car. Lucy watched as they drove away slowly, and then went to get the Subaru.

Alone in the car, she flipped up the visor and leaned forward so she could see the sky. It was the blank, milky white that often signaled a snowstorm. She started the engine and switched on the radio, searching for a weather report.

All she got, though, was varying tones of

static as she drove past the big, substantial clapboard houses that lined Main Street. On one big, snow-covered lawn a group of children, togged out in bright red and blue and green snowsuits, were making a snowman. The scene reminded her of a Christmas card.

If only life was like the paintings, she thought. She loved living in New England — the small towns, the rugged individualists, even the annual town meetings. Self-reliance. Hard work. Thrift. Common sense. Common crackers. She loved it when the kids came in with rosy cheeks, looking like the children in Tasha Tudor books. What had gone wrong, she wondered, pulling up and parking behind Mrs. Asquith's car and watching as Bill helped Lucretia into the house.

She was so absorbed in her thoughts that she never once looked in the rearview mirror, never noticed that she had been followed.

Twenty

The Giant was furious when he realized Jack had stolen his treasure.

On Monday morning the radio announced Gerald's arrest for the theft of Josiah's Tankard:

"Former Winchester College President Gerald Asquith was arrested by state police who allege he stole an antique pewter tankard from the Tinker's Cove Library, placing a copy in its place.

"State police say the theft went unnoticed for years, and was only discovered when the copy was found with the body of Hayden Northcross, who committed suicide last week. A subsequent investigation revealed that Asquith sold the tankard at Sotheby's auction house in New York City, and received more than forty thousand dollars for it."

Stunned at the amount, Lucy dropped the knife she was using to make peanut butter and jelly sandwiches for the kids' lunches, spattering jelly on the floor. She bent down to wipe it up with a paper towel, eagerly listening for more details about the arrest. All she learned, however, was that Gerald would be arraigned that morning.

As Lucy finished packing the lunches she decided she would spend the morning finishing up the gambling story. Ted would undoubtedly want to run it as background for the story about Asquith.

"Bill?" she called up the stairs. "Do me a favor and drop Zoe off at Kiddie Kollege this morning?" She checked the clock, and sent a second message echoing up the stairs: "You've got five minutes 'til the school bus."

"We're always way too early," said Toby, clattering down the stairs and stuffing his lunch into his backpack.

"You always rush us out there," complained Elizabeth, "and then we have to wait in the cold."

"It wouldn't be quite so cold if you wore gloves and a hat and zipped your jacket." Lucy could hear the bus, down at the bottom of the hill. "If you don't get out there this minute, you're going to miss it and I really don't want to drive you this morning. Sara! Get down here! It's the bus."

"You don't have to yell, Mom. I'm right here."

Lucy gave her middle daughter a kiss on the cheek, and a shove toward the door. Then with a sigh of exasperation she watched the three go down the driveway: Toby strode along on his long legs, Sara ran, and Elizabeth did her very best imitation of Tyra Banks on a fashion runway.

Turning back to the sink, Lucy loaded the breakfast dishes into the dishwasher. Then she zipped Zoe into her snowsuit, handed Bill his lunchbox, and gave them each a good-bye kiss. Finally alone in the house, she went straight to the computer.

It was eleven when she was finished; she just had time to drop the story off before she had to pick up Zoe.

"Lucy! I knew you wouldn't let me down," exclaimed Ted, when she pushed open the door to *The Pennysaver* office.

"It's all here," she said, handing him a computer disc. "The greed, the compulsion, the desperation, and the shame."

"Sounds like a B-movie," said Ted.

"Isn't that what this is?" asked Lucy.

"What's happening to nice, quiet Tinker's Cove?"

"I don't know, but I'm not complaining," said Ted. "This sure beats writing about the Cub Scouts' Pinewood Derby."

"I guess," chuckled Lucy, who well remembered long, noisy Sunday afternoons in the church basement when Toby and the other boys in his den raced the little wooden cars they had carved out of blocks of wood. "Did you go to the arraignment this morning?"

"Yeah. It was pretty awful. Gerald looked terrible. He hasn't got a lawyer, yet. The judge entered a not guilty plea for him. No bail, of course."

"They think he'd skip town?"

"Worse. I think they're worried he might kill himself."

Lucy studied the counter between herself and Ted. "Was his wife there?"

"No."

"Poor Gerald."

"Poor Gerald! I'm surprised at you, Lucy. The man stole the town's most valuable artifact — actually pretended he was selling it on behalf of the library — and you feel sorry for him?"

"I do. He couldn't help himself any more than an alcoholic or a drug addict can.

Read my story and you'll understand."

"That doesn't make what he did right," said Ted. "And besides, if he had been on drugs or booze he would've been caught a lot sooner."

"True enough," said Lucy, turning to go. At the door she paused. "Did you talk to Horowitz?"

"He gave the usual press conference."

"I just wondered, did he say anything about Bitsy or Hayden?"

Ted smiled and shook his head. "Not a word, kiddo. Just the contrary. He made a big point of saying that this did not change the status of the Howell and Northcross cases, which are both closed."

Lucy shook her head in disbelief. "I don't get it. We have this little town library and all this stuff is going on: murder, suicide, theft, for Pete's sake, and he's saying there's no connection. That just doesn't make sense." She pushed open the door and marched out, leaving the little bell attached to the top of the door tinkling in her wake.

Once she was out on the sidewalk, Lucy felt as if she needed to burn off some steam. Instead of driving, she decided to walk over to Kiddie Kollege. It was only a few blocks and the fresh air would do her good.

The sun wasn't shining and the sky was still full of clouds, but the temperature was unusually mild. The thermometer outside Slack's Hardware read thirty degrees, a heat wave.

The next shop was the Carriage Trade, a shop that sold expensive, tasteful clothing for women. The four dress forms in the window were bare, except for sandwich boards with the letters S-A-L-E. Lucy smiled, thinking that Sue would no doubt be checking out the bargains if she hadn't already done so.

Maybe she should stop in, too. After all, she loved the sweater Bill had bought here and given her for Christmas. The thought gave her pause; she had last worn the sweater at her first meeting of the library board when she had been so worried about making a good impression.

She smiled grimly at the thought. If only she'd known then what she knew now. The board members weren't quite the up-standing citizens she had once thought. Ed Bumpus was gruff and rude, Corney was plagiarizing recipes for her column, Gerald was a gambler. Who else had a secret, she wondered, a secret that was important enough to kill for?

There was still one board member, she

realized, who she hardly knew. It was about time, she decided, picking up her pace, that she got better acquainted with Chuck Canaday.

Twenty-one

Bambi and all the other animals fled in terror from the flames that were consuming the forest.

As much as Lucy had enjoyed her brisk walk over to Kiddie Kollege, the walk back to retrieve the car convinced her it hadn't been such a good idea. Zoe dragged her feet and dawdled, stopping every few feet to poke a stick into the snow piled alongside the sidewalk.

The balmy temperature didn't seem quite so balmy, either, thanks to a smart breeze. The sign in front of the bank may have read thirty degrees but the wind chill made it feel more like twenty. When Zoe plopped down in the slushy snow to make a snow angel, Lucy lost her temper.

"Zoe! You're going to get soaking wet!" she scolded, lifting the little girl to her feet and carrying her the remaining few feet of sidewalk to the car. "It's lunchtime.

We have to get home."

Lucy strapped her into her booster seat and started the engine, pushing the heater up as high as it would go. It was times like these, she thought, when she wished she lived a bit closer to town.

She drove the familiar route down Main Street on automatic pilot, thinking of what she was going to make for supper, and not paying much attention to the car. She had reached Route One and was speeding along when she first noticed wisps of smoke or steam slipping out from the side of the hood.

Not quite believing what she was seeing, she rubbed her eyes and checked the gauges. The engine temperature was normal, the oil light wasn't on. She slowed down a little bit but that only seemed to make things worse; the smoke was really pouring out now and a car coming the other way flashed its lights and honked at her.

Seeing the turnoff for Red Top Road ahead, she pulled over to the side and stopped the car. She got out to investigate and was horrified to see little orange tongues of flames licking up through the crack between the hood and the fender.

"Oh, no," she exclaimed, yanking open

the back door. With shaking hands she struggled to unfasten Zoe's seat belt, then grabbed the little girl by the upper arms and dragged her out of the car.

"Ow! That hurt!"

"I'm sorry, baby," she crooned, clutching the little one to her breast and backing away from the car. It was then she spotted her purse on the passenger seat.

She dropped Zoe to her feet, ordering her to stay put, and cautiously approached the car. She could feel the heat on her face; the flames were a good six inches long now and black smoke was pouring from the engine. She held her breath and reached into the car, snatching her purse and dashing back to Zoe.

Hearing an ominous whoosh, she grabbed her mittened hand and dragged her away from the car. There was a big pop; Lucy turned and saw the interior burst into a ball of flame.

"Oh, my God," she moaned, collapsing to her knees and clutching Zoe to her.

By now the car was totally involved in flame and the air was filling with thick, black smoke. The acrid stink of burning oil and plastic irritated her nose and throat and made her eyes sting. Lucy coughed and backed even further away, reaching into her purse for her cell phone. When she could breathe a little better she punched in 9-1-1.

"My car's on fire," she told the dispatcher. "I'm at Route One and Red Top Road."

"Is anyone in the car?"

"No. We're out, we're safe," said Lucy, caressing Zoe's cheek and pressing the little girl tight against her hip. She sobbed. "Please hurry."

"They're on the way," said the dispatcher. "Just hold tight and they'll be there in a minute or two."

"Thank you." Tears were rolling down Lucy's face and she was shaking with sobs, unable to take her eyes off the burning car. She was terrified to think what might have happened if she hadn't stopped the car in time. It had all happened so fast; only a few minutes had passed from the moment she first noticed the smoke.

In the distance she could already hear the sirens growing steadily louder as the firetrucks approached. When the engine arrived some of the men immediately began spraying foam on the car and the road; two others approached her.

"Are you all right?" asked the first, a tall man whose face was obscured by the cloth he wore beneath his helmet.

"We're fine," said Lucy, her voice wavering and her face crumpling. "I'm sorry. I just can't seem to stop crying."

"It's shock," said the shorter firefighter, who Lucy was surprised to see was a woman. "It's normal. I'll get you some blankets."

Lucy realized she was shivering, and so was Zoe, and was grateful for the warmth of the orange blankets the firefighters draped over their shoulders. It was only a few minutes later when Barney arrived and bundled them in the back of his cruiser for the drive home.

"What happened, Lucy?"

"I don't know. One minute I was driving home and the next I was standing by the side of the road watching my car burn up."

"Have you had any trouble with it lately?"

"No. I just got the oil changed last month. The mechanic said everything looked fine. It's old, but it's never let me down." It was true, she realized. The Subaru had been like a faithful friend, carrying her and the kids to countless ballet lessons and Cub Scout meetings and swimming classes, hauling tons of groceries home from the IGA, giving her the freedom to come and go in all kinds of weather. "I'm going to miss that car," she said.

"You got a lot of years out of it," sighed Barney.

"Nearly 150,000 miles."

"I guess it deserves a rest, then," said Barney, turning into the driveway. He braked and turned his jowly Saint Bernard face to her. "I've got an accident report to fill out, if you feel up to it."

"Sure," said Lucy, dabbing at her eyes and sniffing. "Actually, I'll be glad of the company. Come on in."

But as she fussed around the kitchen, heating up soup and spreading peanut butter and jelly onto bread for sandwiches for the three of them, Lucy couldn't add much information to what she'd already told Barney. For the life of her, she couldn't figure out what had caused the car to suddenly burst into flames.

After they finished eating, Barney stood up and put on his jacket, then smoothed his hand over his graying crew cut and set his cap on his head. Standing in the kitchen in his regulation black boots, he tapped his clipboard against his leg.

"Listen," he said in a low voice, making sure Zoe couldn't hear, "I don't like the sound of this. Especially with everything that's been going on. I think you should lay low, if you know what I mean."

"What do you mean?" Lucy narrowed her eyes.

"I mean, I think that fire might not o' been an accident. I think it might have been set."

"Oh," said Lucy, suddenly feeling rather weak in the knees and sitting down. It was one thing to harbor a vague suspicion, as she had ever since the near miss when the kids were sledding, but it was another thing altogether to have those suspicions voiced by somebody else, especially if that somebody else happened to be a police officer.

"This is getting really scary," she said, shivering involuntarily and raising tear-filled eyes to Barney. "When I think what could have happened — what if I hadn't gotten Zoe out of the car in time?"

"I didn't mean to upset you," said Barney, who would rather deal with a drunk and disorderly than a crying woman any day. He started to reach for the doorknob, but stopped himself and stood uneasily shifting his weight from one foot to the other.

"All's well that ends well, I guess. But it

wouldn't hurt to be extra careful for a few days." He turned and yanked the door open. "Better safe than sorry, right?"

Twenty-two

*The Fairy Godmother waved her wand again,
and the pumpkin was transformed into
a beautiful coach.*

After Barney left, Lucy dried her eyes and began tidying up the lunch dishes. She appreciated his warning, but at the moment she was concerned with a more immediate problem: how to tell Bill about the car. She was afraid he might not take it well.

But when she finally screwed up her courage to tell him, after making sure he was sitting down with a beer near at hand, he surprised her.

"Lucy, that car doesn't owe us a thing," he said, pulling her down on his lap. "Things are just things, but people are people. All I care about is that you and Zoe are okay." He gave her a squeeze. "It's a good thing you realized something was wrong when you did — it could've been a tragedy."

"I know." Lucy fingered his beard. "But what will I do now? I don't have a car anymore!"

"I'll call the insurance agent tonight," said Bill, patting her knee. "We probably won't get much for the car, but we should get a rental car for a few weeks while we look for something new."

"Really?" Lucy smiled, considering the possibilities.

"Really. Now, where's my supper, woman?"

"It's my morning at the food pantry, so just call the church if you need me." Juanita's breath made a cloud in the frosty morning air as she stood on the doorstep the next morning, dropping Sadie off for a playdate.

"We'll be fine," said Lucy. "Say, can you give me a ride into town when you pick up Sadie?"

"Sure. You've got car trouble?"

"You could say that. The car caught fire yesterday."

"It did? Is everybody all right?"

"Zoe and I got a little scare, that's all."

"You're lucky nobody was hurt. How'd it happen?"

"I wish I knew. The car was going great

until I noticed the smoke." She shook her head. "They tell me it's a complete loss. I'm supposed to pick up a copy of the accident report at the police station, and I have to pick up a rental car. The insurance will pay for it — thank goodness."

"Well, that's one good thing," said Juanita brightly, but her big brown eyes were solemn. "I'll take you wherever you need to go. See you later."

After she left and the girls went upstairs to Zoe's room to play, Lucy decided to give Chuck a call. The sooner she got to the bottom of this mess, she realized, the happier she'd feel.

The motherly voice that answered his phone assured her that Mr. Canaday would certainly be delighted to meet with her, but unfortunately he was not in his office. She might be able to reach him at home, the voice said, rattling off the number. Or on his car phone — Lucy should definitely try that. And of course, she could always dial his pager. That would probably be best.

Lucy hung up and looked at the numbers she had scrawled down on her notepad. She dialed Chuck's home number and got his machine: "You know what to do. Leave a message and I'll get back to you."

She left a message, asking him to call her, and dialed the car phone, but couldn't get through. An operator thanked her for trying but said a connection could not be established at this time.

As a last resort she tried the pager. A recorded voice told her to punch in her phone number, and she did, but doubted Chuck would respond to a number he didn't recognize.

That done, there was nothing to do but wait. In the meantime, she could mix up some cookie dough for the girls. She was just putting it in the refrigerator to chill when the phone rang.

"Lucy, it's Chuck, returning your call."

"Thanks for calling back so quickly," began Lucy. "Something's happened and I'd like to get together with you to discuss the library." An odd thought occurred to her and she digressed. "I mean, Gerald isn't still president, is he?"

"Actually, he is," said Chuck. "I checked the bylaws and we have to have a board meeting and vote on a new president."

"Can we do that? Do we still have a quorum?"

"I'm not sure," admitted Chuck. "I think

we do as long as everybody comes. There are still five of us, right?"

"Yup. You, Corney, Ed, Miss Tilley, and me . . . but I have to tell you I had a close call yesterday."

"What happened?" He sounded genuinely concerned.

"My car burst into flames."

"Jesus, Mary, and Joseph — are you okay?"

"Yup. The car's gone, though."

"Well, that can be replaced." He paused. "I think we better talk. Can you come into the office?"

"Sure, I'm picking up a rental today. Monday, Wednesday, and Friday mornings are best for me."

"How about ten tomorrow — Wednesday morning? If we don't have that storm they're predicting."

"That's fine with me." Lucy paused, then asked, "What storm?"

"It's supposed to be a big nor'easter — but they've been saying that all winter. I swear they do it just to encourage business — everybody runs to the store and stocks up on batteries and stuff and we just get a few more inches of snow."

"Well, I'm keeping my fingers crossed just in case," said Lucy. "See you tomorrow."

"Wow! Valentine cookies," enthused Juanita when she arrived at a little after one. "Did you help?"

Sadie pointed out a particularly large, lopsided heart thickly covered with bright red icing and silver dragées. "I made that one for you."

"For me? It's beautiful! Thank you!"

Lucy smiled as Sadie, beaming with pride, presented her mother with the cookie. "That one is too beautiful to eat, so you'll have to take some of the others, too." She filled a plastic bag with cookies, glancing at Zoe as she worked. She'd been doing the same thing all morning, she realized. It was as if she had to reassure herself that Zoe was really all right.

She handed the bag of cookies to Juanita. "We'll just get our coats, okay?"

"Take your time. I'm not in a rush."

A half hour later, Juanita dropped Lucy and Zoe at the garage. "I don't mind waiting." she offered. "Just in case."

"There's no need. I called this morning and the car's all ready."

"Okay. See ya later . . . and thanks for the cookies."

"Thanks for the ride," said Lucy, waving.

She and Zoe went into the office, where Lucy rang the bell for service. She was just opening her checkbook when a kid with long, blond hair appeared. The name embroidered on his shirt was Gary.

"Hi. I've come to pick up a rental car."

"Okay," he said, flipping through a pile of invoices. "It's Stone, right?"

"Right," she said, holding tight to Zoe's hand so she couldn't wander off in the direction of the vending machines.

"Here we go. It's all set with the insurance company."

"That's great."

"No problem. Hey, that was some fire you had. That car is toast."

"You've seen the car?" asked Lucy.

"Yup. Cops impound all the wrecks with us. OUIs, arrests, they all come here. Want to take a look at it?"

Lucy hesitated, remembering the fear she had felt the day before. "I don't think so," she finally said. "Do you have any idea what caused the fire?"

"Fire marshall's gonna take a look, but I don't think he's gonna be able to tell. There's not much left." Gary grinned at her as he handed over the keys. "You're sure you don't want a souvenir? I pulled the medallion off."

"I guess I would," said Lucy. "Thanks." She took the little chrome ornament representing the constellation Pleiades and tucked it in her pocket, but she kept her eyes straight ahead as she walked to the rental car, a big Buick sedan. She didn't want to see the burned-out hulk of the Subaru.

As she unlocked the car, Lucy thought of what Barney had said. It would be easy enough to set a car on fire; all it would take was a gas-soaked rag thrown onto the radiator. Anybody could do that in a second, especially since she had been using a bungee cord to hold down the hood since the latch had broken a few months ago.

Maybe she was paranoid, she thought as she opened the car door for Zoe, but it seemed as if a lot of things were going wrong all of a sudden. First there was the near miss with the truck when the kids were sledding, and then the fire yesterday. What is it they say, she wondered as she helped Zoe into the back seat — trouble comes in threes?

Not if she could help it, she decided. From now on she was going to have to be more careful. She could no longer take her safety, or the kids' safety, for granted. She was going to have to take precautions, like locking the house and the car, and keeping a closer eye on the kids.

"There's no seat for me!" Zoe complained as Lucy strapped her in.

"That's right. You know, I think you're big enough now that you don't need one. What do you think?"

"I'm a big girl."

"So you are," said Lucy, bending down and kissing her on her head. "Know what? I love my big girl very much."

"I know." Zoe smiled the complacent smile of a secure child who is sure of her parents' love and care.

Lucy gave her knee a little pat and got behind the wheel where she adjusted the seat and the mirrors, then started the motor. The roar of the engine startled her; this car was a lot more powerful than the Subaru. She'd have to drive cautiously or she'd be going far too fast, and without four-wheel drive, she reminded herself as she shifted into drive. She inched her way across the lot to the curb cut and stopped there, checking for traffic. She was glad she did, as a huge dump truck zoomed past, going much faster than the speed limit.

She jumped involuntarily, then gave herself a little shake. Being careful was one thing, but she couldn't go on being terrified all the time. She took her foot off the brake and glided out into the road, accelerating gradually. Tomorrow, she remembered, she'd be seeing Canaday. Maybe together they could get to the bottom of this thing.

Twenty-three

The King and Queen decided it was time for their son, the Prince, to choose a wife.

When Lucy got to Canaday's office the next morning, after leaving Zoe at Kiddie Kollege, she found it was a modern suite located on the second floor of the outlet mall, right above Liz Claiborne and Van Heusen. Canaday wasn't there.

"I'm sorry," said his secretary, a fiftyish woman with permed gray hair and eyeglasses on a string around her neck, "but Chuck's running late. He said he hoped you'd wait — he'll get here just as soon as he can."

"No problem," said Lucy, taking a seat on a rather battered captain's bench and picking up a copy of *People* magazine. She couldn't help staring at the woman; her polyester plaid vest reminded her of someone. "Are you related to Edna Withers?" she finally asked.

"She's my twin sister. I'm Edith and she's Edna, and we're both Withers because we married brothers." Edith looked at her sharply, over her half-glasses. "And we don't ever swap, so don't bother to ask."

"It never occurred to me," said Lucy, her mind boggling at the thought.

"Well, you'd be surprised how many people it does occur to," insisted Edith. "And they don't mind saying so, either."

"So your sister is, I mean was, Bitsy Howell's landlady?"

Edith nodded. "Wasn't that terrible? Her getting shot like that? Right in broad daylight? Gives you the creeps."

"Sure does," said Lucy.

"And then that family of hers — I never heard of such a thing! 'Just give everything to the Salvation Army.' That's what they told Edna. It doesn't seem as if they cared, somehow."

"Did she do that? Give everything away?" Lucy was wondering if she could get a peek at Bitsy's apartment — maybe she could find some sort of clue there.

Edith nodded, dashing her hopes. "I spent all weekend helping her clear out the place. That Bitsy, poor thing, she wouldn't have won any prizes for neatness, I can tell you that. Stuff everywhere. So many books — I guess you'd expect that, her being a librarian. And papers scattered everywhere, lots of them filled with nothing but scribbles and numbers. We filled bags and bags with nothing but garbage. Then there were the clothes — they had to be boxed up. And there were her little bits and pieces, jewelry and a Bible and little oddments, you know what I mean. Those we boxed up and sent to her family, even though they said not to. We couldn't quite throw them away. We just couldn't."

"I think you did the right thing," said Lucy.

"I hope so." Edith reached for a tissue and blew her nose. "We decided to keep the furniture, after all. I told Edna that she might as well because she could raise the rent a little bit for a furnished apartment."

"Might as well," agreed Lucy.

Hearing footsteps in the vestibule, Edith tilted her head toward the door. "That's him, now," she said.

"Hi, Edith. How's every little thing?" asked Chuck, shaking a dusting of snow off his overcoat and hanging it on a rack.

"Just fine, Mr. C." She nodded toward Lucy. "Mrs. Stone is here."

"Lucy! Thanks for waiting." He picked a

stack of letters off the corner of Edith's desk and glanced through them. "Can I offer you something — coffee? Coke?"

"No, thanks."

"Well, come on in my office," he said, opening the door for her. "Edith, no calls, please."

Lucy took a seat opposite Chuck's desk and looked around his office. She'd never seen anything like it — every surface was covered with piles of papers. Folders were even tucked in the bookcases, stuck between the law books, and spilling out of the lower shelf onto the floor.

"Don't mind the mess," he said, waving a hand. "I'm more organized than I look. And I'm awfully glad you called. I'm really concerned about the library. Things were bad enough, and now this business with Gerald . . ."

"It came as a complete surprise?"

"You bet it did. *Shock* is more like it." He propped his elbow on the desk and rested his cheek on his hand, shaking his head. "Mrs. Asquith wants me to defend him, but I had to tell her that it was impossible. I mean, I can't defend him and represent the library's interests, too." He shrugged. "I gave her some names. I hope the DA's not going to be too hard-nosed about this

295

and is willing to work out a deal with Gerald. They could let him make good the loss and give him a suspended sentence."

"Unless," began Lucy, an unbidden thought coming to mind.

"What?"

"I just thought of it. What if Gerald killed Bitsy and Hayden?" said Lucy. "Maybe they figured out that he stole the tankard."

"Gerald? A murderer?" Chuck snorted. "I don't think so."

"Neither do I," agreed Lucy. "But I didn't think he was a gambler, either. Something's at the bottom of this. I mean Bitsy and Hayden, and well, me, too." She set her jaw, looking at him defensively. "I don't think I'm paranoid but I can't help wondering if my car was set on fire on purpose. Being on this board seems to be awfully dangerous. If it isn't the tankard, what could it be?"

Chuck leaned back awkwardly in his chair and scratched his head, mussing up his hair. "Listen, if you want to quit, I'll understand," he said.

For a second, Lucy was tempted. "No," she said. "If someone's trying to scare me off, they picked the wrong person. I don't like being scared. It just makes me mad."

Chuck grinned. "Well, if you're determined to stick it out, can I ask a favor?"

"Anything."

"Do you think you could ask your husband to look at some figures for me? He's a contractor, isn't he? He knows about construction costs, right? He'd know if something was out of line or not, wouldn't he?"

"I guess so."

Chuck began rummaging through the papers on his desk. "See, I'm having a problem with the figures for the library addition. We all got that final accounting at the meeting, and everything looked fine. But after Bitsy was killed I copied all the files in her computer — just to be safe, you know. Just a precaution. And when I was going through them, well, I noticed that her figures didn't match the final accounting." He stopped shifting the papers around and looked at Lucy. "I'm not saying it means anything. After all, I don't know what her figures were based on. Were they estimates? Were they from invoices? I don't know, and I don't have time to really go into it. But I do know that with Gerald's arrest, Horowitz is going to be asking for the books and I want to know what's in them."

"Bill's not doing much these days," ad

mitted Lucy, "because of the weather. I don't think he'd mind. But you know he's already checked the figures for Ed. Everything looked okay to him."

"I know. I wouldn't even think of asking him except for all that's happened."

"It's worth a try," said Lucy, doubtfully.

Chuck poked through a few more files and shook his head helplessly. "Edith!" he yelled. "Where are those library figures?"

She bustled in and zeroed in on the credenza, deftly producing a thick file.

"What would I do without you?" asked Chuck, taking it from her.

Edith smiled at him and clucked her tongue. "You really need to tidy up this office." She sounded just like a mother telling her son to clean up his room.

"I'll do it tomorrow," he said, leafing through the folder.

"I've heard that before," said Edith, going back to her desk.

Chuck looked up and smiled at Lucy, inviting her to share his amusement. She couldn't resist and broke into a smile, too.

"You know, I stopped in at the library — that's why I was late, in fact," said Chuck. "I thought that with all this upset things might be topsy-turvy. But they weren't.

The new librarian has everything running smoothly."

Lucy nodded. "It's amazing, isn't it? The board's a shambles but it's business as usual in the library. Makes you wonder if we're really needed, doesn't it?"

"I guess somebody has to sign the checks," observed Chuck. "Thanks for this." He gave her the folder. "And be careful. We can't keep losing board members at this rate or we won't have a quorum."

She was sure he meant it as a joke, but it rattled her. Clutching the folder, she hurried out the door and into the hallway, almost bumping into Corney, who was wearing a hat and scarf in a becoming shade of blue that emphasized her eyes, and was carrying a large box, wrapped in a big red ribbon.

"A valentine for Chuck?" asked Lucy, with a big smile.

"Not really," said Corney, her face reddening. For once she seemed embarrassed. "Actually, he did some work for me, saved me from a bad situation and, well, this is just my way of saying thanks."

"I'm sure he'll appreciate it," said Lucy, giving her a little wave and heading down the stairs.

The lingering almond aroma left no doubt in Lucy's mind that Chuck was going to receive a big box of madeleines. Lucy wondered if it was really a thank-you present; hadn't Sue mentioned something about a big lawsuit involving Corney?

Pushing open the door, Lucy saw that snow had started to fall. Forgetting all about her resolution to be more careful, she dashed across the parking lot to the car, never noticing the big, black pick-up truck that was just turning in. Never slowing, it rounded the line of parked cars and pulled up behind the Buick, blocking it in.

Lucy's heart leapt to her mouth, but when she looked up she saw it was only Ed.

"Hi, Lucy. How's it going?"

"Fine." Lucy nodded, stepping up to the cab of the truck. "Looks like we're going to get that storm after all."

"Yeah," agreed Ed. "The wind's pickin' up already. S'posed to be one hell of a blow."

"And we've got a high tide and a full moon. There could be flooding."

"Well, you're high and dry there on old Red Top. You don't have to worry." He glanced curiously at the folder she was holding. "What'cha got there? Library business?"

"Oh, no." Lucy found herself reluctant to admit the truth. "It's just some legal papers for Bill — a disgruntled customer."

"Wouldn't expect he'd have that sort of problem," drawled Ed.

"Some people are never satisfied," shrugged Lucy, backing away from the truck. "Do you mind moving? I've got to get to the IGA before the storm gets any worse."

"Sure," said Ed, touching the bill of his cap in a polite farewell. "Didn't realize that was your car. Thought you had a little rice burner. Did something happen to it?"

"I had an accident," said Lucy, unwilling to go into details.

"That's too bad." Ed scratched his chin. "Maybe you'd better be more careful."

"I sure will," said Lucy, giving him a little wave and climbing into the Buick. She laid the folder down beside her without a glance and settled herself behind the wheel. It was only when she turned to check that everything was clear, before backing up, that she noticed the big magic marker letters on the folder. They spelled out two words: "Library Addition."

And they must, she realized, have been

clearly visible to Ed while she stood chatting with him, the folder clutched to her chest. All the time they were talking he must have known she had lied to him. Why had she done it? She didn't really know. It was just one of those stupid things that get people in trouble, she thought, hoping that by some miracle Ed hadn't noticed.

With more force than was necessary, she jammed the car into gear and reversed out of her parking spot, reminding herself to accelerate cautiously on the increasingly slippery road surface. Now, with a storm coming on, was no time to have an accident.

Twenty-four

Many years went by and a thicket of briars grew up and surrounded the Enchanted Castle.

The snow was falling thickly by the time the older kids got home from school and several inches had already accumulated.

"No school tomorrow," crowed Toby as he unzipped his jacket.

"Don't be so sure," cautioned Lucy. "The forecasters have been wrong before."

"It was on the loudspeaker," said Sara. "The principal said no school tomorrow because of the snow emergency."

"Really?" Lucy had never heard of this happening before. She went into the family room and switched on the TV, flipping to the weather channel. She waited impatiently while weather conditions in foreign capitals were reported and a batch of commercials were aired. When the broadcast resumed an earnest young woman in a bright blue suit assured her that gale force winds, freezing temperatures, and a record snowfall were expected to batter the entire Northeast. Just in case she had any doubts, the satellite weather map showed an enormous swirling mass just offshore.

"The National Weather Service has announced a storm warning for Northern New England, and a storm watch is in effect for Rhode Island and Connecticut right on down to New York City," recited the weather girl. "This is a massive storm with serious destructive power and it is being watched closely. Flooding is expected in coastal communities and public safety officials are planning to evacuate some areas. Businesses and schools have been urged to close tomorrow and anyone whose job is not considered essential for public safety is encouraged to remain at home."

"Will we be okay?" asked Sara.

"Sure," said Lucy. "This old house has been through lots of storms."

"I bet we'll lose electricity," grumbled Elizabeth. "I hate that. It's so boring."

"It's not so bad," said Lucy. "What is it Daddy says? We'll have to watch TV by candlelight?"

Elizabeth rolled her eyes and groaned. "Right, Mom."

"In the meantime, you can all get to work bringing in some wood for the stoves. Fill all the woodboxes and stack as much as you can on the porch, okay?"

"Do we have to?" asked Toby.

"Not if you don't mind freezing to death — get to work, all of you. Now."

While the kids were busy with the wood, Lucy checked her food supplies. She had bought extra milk and bread that morning, and the freezer and pantry were full. A frozen turkey caught her eye, and she took it out of the freezer to thaw, planning to cook it tomorrow. The oven — thank goodness it was gas — would help keep the kitchen warm.

The flashlights all had fresh batteries, as did the radio, and they had plenty of candles and a couple of oil lamps. She set them all on the kitchen counter. Congratulating herself for remembering, she plugged her cell phone into the charger. After that there wasn't anything else to do so she went out to help the kids.

When Bill came home he had an enormous heart-shaped box of chocolates for Lucy and a bunch of flowers from the florist shop.

"You shouldn't have," exclaimed Lucy,

throwing her arms around his neck and nuzzling his beard.

"I didn't want you to be disappointed. I know how much you were looking forward to going out to dinner, but it doesn't look as if that's going to happen. They're saying snow right through tomorrow."

"And then there's the digging out — that's going to take a while," said Lucy, pulling away from Bill and starting to arrange the flowers in a vase. "Oh, well, there's always next year. Besides, we've got everything we need right here."

"That's right," agreed Bill, stepping up behind her and wrapping his arms around her waist. "You're everything I need."

"And I do have the chocolates," said Lucy, leaning back against him.

"Tease," he whispered, biting her ear.

Lucy turned around and raised her face for a kiss, but thought better of it when she heard Toby clattering down the back stairs. She stepped away from Bill with a sigh.

"What's for dinner?" Toby asked, poking his head into the kitchen.

"Lasagna," said Lucy, opening the oven. "The lasagna of love."

Toby looked from his mother to his father, a puzzled expression on his face. Spotting the box of chocolates, he asked, "Hey, can

I have some of that candy?"

"No! That's my present and I haven't even opened the box yet."

Seeing Toby's disappointment, she immediately felt bad. She always shared her Valentine's Day candy; it was a family tradition. "After supper — but I get the square ones," she added.

That evening, Lucy asked Bill if he would look at the library figures. He took the file, but never opened it, opting instead to play some computer games with the kids. "We're bound to lose power soon," he said, "and there's no telling how long it will be before we get it back."

But although the wind howled all night, occasionally slamming the house with such strong gusts that the walls shook and the pictures swayed on their hooks, the electricity was still on in the morning.

"It's because it's such light, powdery snow," said Bill, sipping his coffee and looking out the kitchen window.

"It's just a matter of time," said Lucy, stirring the oatmeal. "All it takes is for one tree to get blown down on the wires."

"Is the snow deep?" asked Zoe, rubbing her eyes sleepily.

"At least a foot, and there's more to

come," said Bill, scooping her up for a hug. "Happy Valentine's Day!"

The storm was already being called the Valentine's Day Blizzard when Lucy checked the weather channel after breakfast. Toby and Elizabeth were sleeping the morning away but Sara and Zoe were busy making Valentines out of construction paper and doilies.

Lucy had plenty to do, too. She had mixed up some cornbread for turkey stuffing and while it was baking had started a batch of cupcakes. Rummaging in a drawer, she found some paper liners printed with hearts and set them in the tins, carefully filling them with chocolate batter. The girls could ice them later — they'd love decorating them with candy.

Bill, however, was restless. Unable to go to work, he wandered from window to window, looking out at the storm. "No sense shoveling," he said. "It's drifting too much. Might as well wait 'til it stops." Cooped up in the house, he flipped channels nervously. Regular programming had been cancelled; the stations were competing to have the latest news on the record-breaking blizzard.

Periodically, he'd give her a report. "The

entire Northeast is shut down, even the stock market." A few minutes later: "Terrible flooding in Cape Cod. Houses gone in Chatham, terrific damage to the National Seashore beaches." Off he'd go, only to return with more news. "Fifty-foot seas — they say a Liberian tanker is in trouble off Nantucket. The Coast Guard's on the way, but they're not holding out much hope."

"You're making me nervous," said Lucy. "Can't you find something to do?"

"Sorry," he said. "You probably don't want to hear about the tragic fire in Fall River."

"You're right, I don't," said Lucy, tipping the cornbread out onto a wire rack. "How'd you like to chop up some onions? You know how they make me cry."

"Sure," he said eagerly. "How many? Ten? Twelve?"

"Two."

"I can do more."

"The recipe says two."

"Okay," he said, setting the chopping board on the counter. "Mind if I take a look at that recipe?"

While Bill made the stuffing, Lucy poured herself another cup of coffee. She sat down at the kitchen table to keep him company.

"Have you had a chance to look at those library figures yet?" she asked.

"Not yet," said Bill, who was carefully slicing the cornbread into cubes.

"Do you know what to look for?"

"Not exactly — I'm no accountant. But since the guy who was writing the checks has turned out to be a compulsive gambler, it seems logical to look for inflated costs. That might mean he was getting kickbacks."

"That would mean somebody else was involved — the subcontractors, right?"

"Yeah," agreed Bill, thunking a frying pan onto the stove and popping in a cube of butter. When it had finished sizzling, he added the onion and stirred it around. "When you think about it, this wasn't Gerald's first construction project. As president of the college he was responsible for several new buildings. I bet he's done this before, and knows just which subcontractors will play ball with him. That was one of the first things I was going to look for — see if he's been using the same contractors on a number of projects."

"But I thought Ed was in charge of the library addition."

"As I understand it, he was keeping an eye on the day-to-day progress. Making sure that the actual construction was being done right, that they were using the right materials. Gerald was in charge of the checkbook." He snorted, dumping the onions into the bowl of corn bread and mixing them together. "Kind of like putting the fox in charge of the chicken coop, when you think of it. Now you have to take it from here," he said, handing her the bowl of stuffing. "There's no way I'm going to get intimate with a turkey."

"Okay," laughed Lucy.

The storm continued through the afternoon. Toby and Elizabeth woke around one o'clock and immediately began fighting over who would get the first shower. Toby won and was making himself a fried egg, cheese, and bologna sandwich when Elizabeth appeared in the kitchen.

"That's disgusting — do you know what that does to your arteries?" asked Elizabeth, popping half of an English muffin into the toaster.

"I don't care," said Toby, setting the hot pan in the sink and filling it with water, creating a cloud of steam. "At least I'm not anorexic."

"I'm not anorexic — I eat plenty," insisted Elizabeth.

"Half of an English muffin isn't much of a breakfast," said Lucy. "How about some cereal or yogurt?"

Elizabeth exhaled noisily and rolled her eyes. "I can figure out what I want to eat for myself, thank you very much."

"Fine." Lucy looked out the window at the blowing snow, which had drifted against the shed, practically covering it. She wished she hadn't joined Toby's bandwagon by urging Elizabeth to eat more breakfast — she knew Elizabeth was terrified of getting fat and telling her to eat more would only be met with stubborn resistance. Lucy's plan so far had been to keep tabs on her daughter's daily intake and when it dropped too low, instead of nagging, she made one of her favorite foods. When even this didn't work she had a secret weapon: an imported chocolate and hazelnut spread loaded with fat and calories that Elizabeth couldn't resist.

"I made some cupcakes — maybe you could help Sara and Zoe frost them," she suggested.

"Okay." Elizabeth was finished with breakfast. She slipped her plate into the sink, whirled around, and tapped Toby on the shoulder. "Your turn to do the dishes," she crowed, beating a hasty retreat.

Toby sprang to his feet to chase her, but Lucy intervened. "Load the dishwasher. I'll make sure she does them next time."

"Mom," he wailed, beginning to protest, then changed his mind when Lucy gave him a sharp look. "Okay."

The house seemed to shrink as the afternoon wore on. Toby and Elizabeth couldn't be in the same room without squabbling, and even normally placid Sara and Zoe began to bicker. The wind and snow were still coming down at four, but Bill dragged Toby outside to shovel anyway. "Might as well get a start," he said. "Besides, you've been sitting at that computer all day. You could use some exercise."

"Aw, Dad," groaned Toby. "Do I have to? I'm doing research for a paper."

Bill looked over his shoulder. "What's your paper on? The MTV website? Get a move on."

Toby gave a huge sigh as he logged off, prompting Lucy to wonder for the millionth time why teenagers were so lazy. Given their druthers, he and Elizabeth would sleep well past noon every day; then they would shower for an hour or two before settling down with the computer or

TV. They only showed signs of life when the telephone rang; otherwise they were content to recline and nibble — Toby on any sort of fatty snack food, Elizabeth on her nails.

Hearing high-pitched screams in the kitchen, Lucy went to investigate. She found Sara and Zoe at the kitchen table, which was littered with cupcakes, a bowl of pink frosting, and numerous containers of cake decorations. Zoe's face was red and she was crying.

"What's the matter?"

"Sara took all the silver ones!" Zoe was furious. Lucy had never seen her so upset.

"There were hardly any, Mom. See?" Sara held up a cupcake with a few silver dragées on top.

"You and Sadie used them up on the cookies. Remember?"

"I hate Sadie."

"No, you don't," said Lucy, patting her littlest daughter's shoulder. "It's been a long day. I bet you're tired."

Zoe sniffed and gave a little shudder.

"How about some chocolate sprinkles instead?"

Zoe shook her head.

"I know — wait one minute." Lucy took the big heart-shaped box of chocolates down from the top of the refrigerator, where she had hidden it after the family binge the night before, and opened it up. Inside, nestled among the remaining chocolates, was a heart-shaped piece of chocolate wrapped in red foil. She plucked it out and gave it to Zoe. "How about this?"

Sara gasped, suitably impressed and obviously jealous.

Zoe glanced at her and stuck the candy on top of one of the cupcakes. "This one is mine."

"You can have it for dessert," promised Lucy. "Where's Elizabeth? I thought she was going to help you."

"On the phone. She had to talk to Lance," volunteered Sara, spotting an opportunity to get her big sister in trouble.

She was doomed to be disappointed. "Oh, well," said Lucy. "Let's finish here and I'll help you clean up. You girls did a really good job — these cupcakes are beautiful. We're going to have a lovely Valentine's Day Blizzard supper."

Zoe giggled and licked her fingers.

Lucy was wiping off the table when Toby came in, covered with snow from head to toe.

"Look at you!" exclaimed Lucy, hurrying

over to help him out of his snow-caked clothes. "Where's your Dad?"

"Mr. Bumpus came by and Dad went with him."

"He did?" Lucy was tugging at one of Toby's boots. "Why?"

"Something about the snow load on the library — he said they needed to shovel the roof."

"Shovel the roof?"

Toby ran his fingers through his damp hair. His face was red and flushed and little droplets of water were sparkling on his eyelashes. "It's something out there, Mom. There's a *lot* of snow."

Lucy peered out the window in the kitchen door. Because of the storm it was already starting to get dark, and the snow was still falling heavily, blowing this way and that. Everything was white. The car and truck were mounds of snow sitting in the windswept driveway. The wind had also cleared the front of the shed while covering one side with a huge drift. The same thing had happened to the house; some windows were half-covered with snow, others were bare.

"I wish he hadn't gone," said Lucy. "This isn't any sort of weather to be out in."

"Mr. Bumpus said the road isn't too bad, and he's got four-wheel drive."

"Four-wheel drive has its limits," said Lucy.

Toby was shocked at this heresy. "Don't worry, Mom. They'll be fine. That truck is . . ." He couldn't find words to adequately describe Ed's truck and sputtered. "Cool," he finally said.

"I hope he's back in time for dinner," said Lucy, opening the oven to check the turkey.

"Boy, that smells good," said Toby, spreading some peanut butter on a piece of bread.

"Save some room for dinner," said Lucy as she basted the turkey. "I don't get it — that roof is supposed to have steel beams. I remember people asked about the roof when they first presented the plans at the town meeting."

"Mmmph," said Toby, his mouth full of peanut butter.

Lucy closed the oven door and stood for a minute by the sink, tapping it with the turkey baster. Suddenly dropping it in the sink, she rushed up the back stairs, heading for Bill's little attic office under the eaves. There, she found the folder with the library figures on his desk.

Pulling out the chair, she sat down and opened it, slowly leafing through the pages. She wasn't sure what she was looking for — there were so many figures. After pages and pages of tightly noted columns, she turned with relief to the invoices for materials, neatly clipped together. One of the first was from A-B Steel, she noted with relief. That meant they did use steel beams, the way they were supposed to.

She was about to replace the invoices in the file when she noticed a notebook tucked among the papers — it was the journal kept by the clerk of the works. The clerk of the works, she knew, was responsible for logging in all the deliveries, and he had. Each page was dated and the time for each delivery was noted, as well as the materials. Perilli Excavating, Cove Ready-mix, Tinker's Cove Lumber, O'Brien Plumbing and Heating, Ashley Roofing, Flambeau Millwork — it was all there, a steady stream of deliveries by building materials dealers. But there was no mention of the company she was looking for: A-B Steel.

That didn't mean anything, she told herself. Maybe it was delivered by a hauler with a different name. So she began studying the lists of items. Cubic yards of concrete, squares of shingles, board feet of lumber, windows and doors, nails and wire and pipe, joist hangers, things she recognized and things she didn't. But nowhere was there mention of any steel beams. No I-beams, nothing. But there was a notation of eight forty-foot eight-by-eight beams from the St. Lawrence Salvage Company.

She thought of the open floor plan of the addition, how the circulation desk and the new books area seemed to flow right on into the children's area. There were no walls, no supporting beams. It was one huge, uninterrupted space, about forty feet from the front door to the back wall. Forty feet of roof, now covered with tons of snow, supported not by tempered steel I-beams but by wood beams from a salvage company.

Lucy was no engineer, but she could see why Ed was worried. If she'd known, she would have been worried, too. She reached for the phone, intending to call Chuck, when the lights went out.

That didn't necessarily mean the phone was out, too, she told herself. She lifted the receiver to her ear; there was no dial tone.

Sitting alone in the dark, she pictured Ed's face. The bristling eyebrows, the little piggy eyes. The smile that could seem friendly and open or vaguely threatening. What had he said at the funeral? "I want people to know that Bill Stone signed off on this project, that Bill Stone said it was okay."

She hadn't liked it when he said it then, and she liked it even less now. Bill, she knew, had taken Ed's word that everything was as it should be. He had signed the papers, but he hadn't been involved in the construction. But now, if something was wrong, he could be blamed.

Even worse, thought Lucy, what if something happened to him? Shoveling off a roof was dangerous. A knot formed in her stomach. What if he fell? She felt as if something was gripping her heart; she couldn't breathe. She forced herself to inhale and exhale.

That's why Bitsy died, and Hayden, too. They had made the same discovery she had — that Ed had substituted inferior materials in the library addition. Bitsy must have been working on the figures before the meeting, that's why she had to be killed. Ed hadn't gone to the men's room as he had claimed; he'd gone around the building, let himself into the workroom with his key, and shot Bitsy. He probably hadn't thought twice about it — as a hunter he was used to killing and he didn't think much of Bitsy anyway.

Hayden, also, had been worried about the library. His last words to Ralph had been that there was something he wanted to straighten out. If he had gone to Ed with his questions, Ed wouldn't have hesitated to kill him. He despised Hayden for being gay; he probably thought he was doing everybody a favor. Stealing the tankard and leaving it with Hayden's body had been cunning — it gave Hayden a motive for supposedly killing Bitsy and himself.

And that's why Ed had dragged Bill off to shovel the roof, thought Lucy. Now that Gerald had been arrested, the state police would certainly be taking a close look at the bookkeeping for the addition. Gerald was safe in jail — Ed couldn't get to him. Even worse, realized Lucy, Ed knew that she had the figures — he'd seen her with the folder. Furthermore, he knew that Bill would be taking another look at them. But if Bill died, Ed could blame him for the discrepancies and there'd be nobody to dispute his story.

Nobody but Lucy, and Ed had been doing his very best to frighten the wits out of her. He probably thought that between the sledding incident and the car fire she would be afraid of her own shadow. If he thought that was true, she decided, he didn't know her very well.

She jumped to her feet, banging her head on the slanted ceiling. Wincing at the pain, she clutched her head and groped her way to the door. If only she could get help for Bill. Damn the stupid phone. And the lights, too. Why did they have to go out now? Thank God she still had the cell phone. She could use that, she thought, grasping a knob. She pulled, intending to open the door, but discovered too late that she had instead opened the cabinet where Bill stored his rolled-up plans. Cardboard tubes rained down on her; she tried to turn away, toward the door, but her feet got tangled. The next thing she knew she was flat on her stomach in the pitch black darkness, with a pounding headache.

"Dammit," she muttered, frustrated at the absurdity of her situation — helpless in the dark in her own house with her children only a few rooms away.

Twenty-five

"I'll huff and I'll puff and I'll blow your house in," said the Wolf.

After a minute or two she cautiously felt around in the darkness with her hands, pushing the tubes out of her way and crawling toward the door. She found the knob, the right one this time, and pulled it open.

"Help!" she screamed down the pitch-black stairs. "I'm stuck in the attic." The effort made her head throb.

There was no answer. Alone in the dark, at the top of the steep stairs, she might as well have been in an empty house.

"Toby!" she yelled. "Bring me a flash-light!"

The house was silent.

"Kids," she muttered, feeling her way down the stairs backwards, on her hands and knees. What could they be doing? Were they sitting like idiots, staring at the blank TV screen? They knew better. They should be lighting the oil lamps and checking to see if everyone was okay. Especially their mother.

When she pushed open the door to the second floor hall, Lucy was relieved to see there was still a little daylight filtering in through the windows. She groped her way downstairs to the kitchen. There she lit a lamp and looked for the cell phone, intending to call Barney at the police station to get help for Bill. But the place on the counter where she had left it, freshly charged next to the lamps, was empty. It was gone.

"Where's the cell phone?" she hollered, pushing open the door to the family room. There she saw Toby and the younger girls sitting on the floor, huddled around a lamp, playing checkers. Elizabeth was lounging on the couch, the cell phone in her hand.

"Give that to me," said Lucy, snatching it out of her hand.

"Okay — but it isn't working."

"What do you mean?"

"It was working fine, but then it started making a lot of static and I couldn't hear anymore."

"How long were you using it?" Lucy

grabbed the phone and pushed the power button. The display panel read "Low Bat".

"A while, I guess. Not long."

"I charged it yesterday." Lucy was furious. "You must have been talking for hours. What were you using it for, anyway? This is for emergencies."

"It *was* an emergency," insisted Elizabeth indignantly. "Toby had the phone line tied up with the computer and I had to talk to Lance."

"How could you be so irresponsible?" Lucy's head was spinning. She glared at her daughter, her eyes glittering in the lamplight. "Do you know what you've done?" she began, then broke off. What was the point? Arguing with Elizabeth wasn't going to change the situation.

Her hands shaking with anger and blinking back tears of pain and frustration, Lucy carried her lamp into the bathroom and took three ibuprofen. Then she went back to the kitchen and sat at the table, her head in her hands. She could hear the turkey spitting and hissing in the oven; it must be almost ready.

She took a few deep breaths to calm herself and tried to analyze the situation. Had she overreacted? Was Bill really in danger?

Then she remembered Bitsy, lying on

the floor of the storeroom, her lifeless eyes staring up at the ceiling. She thought of Hayden, his murder cleverly arranged to look like suicide.

She closed her eyes. Bill had gone to meet Bumpus, unaware that he was walking into a trap. Up on the roof it would be easy to rig an accident. One slip and Bumpus would silence Bill forever. Then he'd be able to shift the blame for the shoddy materials onto Bill. It would be his word against that of a dead man.

Lucy shuddered. It might already be too late.

No, she decided, looking out the window at the fading light. That's why Bumpus came along when he did. He'd wait until it was dark. There was still time if she hurried.

Lucy and Toby stepped off the back porch into a bleak wilderness of snow and wind. Clinging together, they hung on to the clothesline and struggled across the short distance to the shed. The snow was so thick that the porch light did little good; its soft glow served only to mark the warmth and safety they were leaving behind as they ventured out in the darkness and howling wind.

Reaching the shed, they scrambled into its shelter, knocking rakes and shovels aside.

"Mom — let me go," said Toby, already panting from the exertion of pulling the frozen door open. His jacket and snowpants were already coated with snow.

Lucy was beginning to doubt the wisdom of her plan. She hadn't realized the strength of the storm. She also wasn't sure of her ability to handle the snowmobile; until now she'd only been a passenger, riding behind Bill.

But Bill was out in the storm, alone with a murderer. She couldn't begin to explain it to Toby — this irrational, irresistible tug. She had to get to him.

"Help me get this thing out and we'll see what happens," she said, tugging at the machine's grab bar. "Chances are I'll meet one of the plows before I get too far."

They both knew the town trucks were equipped with radios; if she reached a truck they could radio for help.

"What makes you so sure the plows are out?" demanded Toby. "They're probably waiting 'til the storm's over."

Lucy knew he was probably right. The DPW superintendent wasn't going to put his men, or his trucks, in danger. Frustrated, she challenged him.

"Are you going to help me or what?"

Toby joined her and together they dragged the snowmobile to the door. He gave the cord a yank and it started right up. Lucy gave him a quick peck on the cheek before she pulled on her helmet and climbed aboard. Then, cautiously, she maneuvered the machine down the ramp and started across the yard to the road. She was halfway there when it sputtered and stalled.

She tried to restart it, but nothing happened. Tears sprang to her eyes and she pounded the useless hunk of metal with her fists.

Toby materialized out of the swirling snow, pounding on his chest to indicate that he would drive. Lucy obediently slid back and he climbed on in front of her. The machine sprang to life once more and she wrapped her arms around his waist and hung on as they hurled forward.

The headlight only showed a wall of whirling white snow but with Toby driving they moved ahead steadily and reached the road. There, Toby cautiously accelerated and they skimmed along the freshly fallen powder. The roar of the wind was muffled by the helmet, but the sudden crack of a falling tree made her start.

Out in the dark emptiness Lucy felt she and Toby were very alone. If anything happened to them it would be a very long time before help came.

She pushed those thoughts from her mind. They couldn't give up; they had to get help for Bill. She swallowed hard as Toby carefully maneuvered the turn at the bottom of Red Top Hill where her car had burned. How far was it to town? Four or five miles at most, a matter of ten or fifteen minutes.

Sensing the open road ahead, Toby accelerated the snowmobile and they surged forward, speeding along through the wild night. Lucy's hands and feet were getting cold; she didn't have the benefit of the heated handles and the warmth of the engine as Toby did. She flexed her fingers and wiggled her toes inside her boots. A sudden flash of light made her jump. It was a broken power line giving off showers of sparks. Toby gave it a wide berth and pushed on.

They passed the Quik-Stop without realizing it. The familiar sign was covered with snow and the gas pumps were simply odd, snow-covered shapes. The first thing they recognized was the church, and next to it was the police station. It wasn't until they pulled up by the steps that they could see the faint blue light of the lamps by the door.

Lucy started to dismount but her legs wouldn't cooperate. They felt heavy and clumsy. She leaned heavily on Toby's shoulders and willed herself to move. Grabbing the railing, she pulled herself up the steps and yanked the door open, practically falling on the floor in front of the dispatcher's desk.

"Good God — what are you doing out on a night like this?" demanded Barney.

Lucy tugged at the helmet but couldn't get it off. Barney came around the desk and eased it off her head. "Easy now," he said. "Tell me what's the matter."

"I need help. Bill's in trouble."

"Jeez. What's happened?"

"He went with Bumpus. To shovel snow off the roof. Of the library." Lucy was struggling to be coherent. "He's the murderer."

Barney stared at her, trying to understand.

"You think Bill's in danger?"

Lucy nodded. "We have to help him."

Barney's face drooped. "Lucy — there isn't anything I can do."

"What do you mean? You can go over there with me!"

"I can't leave the station." Barney looked stricken.

"Well, call for help."

"I can't. There's nobody to call. We've had one emergency after another. You'll just have to wait until somebody gets back. And there's a coupla calls ahead of you." He looked down at the floor and studied the gray and white tiles. "Besides, if what you say is true, it's probably too late."

Lucy slowly blinked her eyes, then turned to retrieve her helmet.

"What do you think you're doing?"

"This is a waste of time. Toby's out there, freezing his ass off. We're going to the library." Lucy pulled the helmet over her head and turned to go.

"Please, Lucy. You're in no shape to go and I bet Toby's no better. Stay here where it's warm and safe. What do you think you're gonna do when you get there?"

She shook her head stubbornly. "I have to go," she said and staggered the short distance across the lobby to the door. She pushed it open and found herself once again in the storm. The wind had quieted, however, and the snow was falling less heavily. Moving stiffly, hanging on to the railing, she slid down the steps and staggered to the snowmobile. She grabbed Toby's shoulders and swung her leg over the seat. As soon as she sat down he was underway, zooming down Main Street to the library.

In minutes they were pulling up beside Bumpus's big black truck, the only one in the parking lot. Lucy tilted her head and raised her eyes to the roof.

There, a work light had been rigged, making an island of brightness in the darkness. She lifted her visor and gasped, seeing two figures struggling near the edge of the roof.

Toby followed her gaze.

She grabbed his arm with her hand as they watched the two dark shadows grapple with each other, locked in a life or death struggle. At first they seemed equally matched but gradually, the slighter, more slender man appeared to be losing ground. As they watched, he was pushed inexorably toward the edge of the roof by the bulkier one. She held her breath.

"No, no, no," she whispered.

She felt Toby tense, and she held his hand in both of hers. As they clung together they saw one of the figures topple off the roof.

Fueled by adrenaline, Lucy leaped off the snowmobile and ran through the snow toward the motionless figure crumpled on the ground.

"Don't let it be Bill," she prayed, kneeling beside the form in the snow. She tugged at the hood covering his face and moaned, recognizing Bill's beard. With her teeth she ripped her glove off and felt his neck for a pulse. It was there — she was sure she felt it.

Suddenly frantic, heart pounding, she looked for help and saw Toby running toward her.

"We have to get him to the hospital."

Toby pointed to the roof, where Bumpus was looking down on Bill's broken body in triumph.

"You'll pay for this!" Lucy yelled, shaking her fist at him. "I saw you. I know who you are."

Bumpus gave no sign of having heard her and turned away.

Lucy brushed the snow from Bill's face. Hearing a moan, she leaned closer to his lips. It wasn't from him, she realized, as the sound grew louder. She froze.

"Listen," she said.

Alerted, Toby turned toward the building.

The sound was insistent, penetrating.

She followed Toby's gaze, realizing with horror that they were hearing the groan of overburdened timbers yielding to the weight of the snow.

"Get down!" she screamed and Bumpus turned to face her. His face was white in the spotlight and his mouth made an "O" as he realized the danger. He seemed to move in slow motion, stumbling as he scrambled across the snowy roof to the ladder that would lead him to safety.

He never reached it. There was a horrible crack, like an explosion. For a moment it seemed as if everything would be all right. Then, with a sudden sucking noise, almost like a huge intake of breath, the roof gave way. Lucy and Toby saw Bumpus teeter on the edge and then he was gone.

They heard a single, piercing scream and then it was quiet.

A few tiny snowflakes were still falling as Toby pointed to the sky. Lucy looked up, and saw faint pinpricks of light.

"Stars," said Toby, bending to help her with Bill. "The storm's over."

"I can't believe it," said Lucy, involuntarily clapping her hand to her head. "I forgot all about the turkey."

Twenty-six

Thirsty and weighted down with stones, the Wolf dragged himself to the well for a drink but when he reached for the bucket he fell right in.

As often happens after a storm, the next day dawned bright and clear. The temperature was a balmy 20 degrees, the sky was cloudless and bright blue. The sunshine was dazzling against the fresh snow; you had to squint to see.

Lucy and Bill were back at the library, ostensibly to survey the damage, but also drawn by the need to see the site of Bill's near-fatal adventure.

"You fell from there," said Lucy, pointing to the corner of the addition high above them.

"I was sure lucky I fell into a snowdrift," said Bill, with the stunned amazement of one who has survived a close call.

"You sure were — especially if you think

of all the stuff that's under that snow — concrete blocks, scraps of wood and pipe." She squeezed his arm. "I've never been so terrified."

He wrapped his arm around her shoulder. "It just wasn't my time, I guess."

They stood in silence for a moment, aware that Ed Bumpus hadn't been nearly as lucky as Bill. He was still inside the shell of the addition, trapped beneath tons of rubble. Searchers were combing through the mess looking for him, but no one expected to find him alive.

"That was some night," said Ted Stillings, joining them and opening his camera bag. "They're calling it the storm of the century, you know. Power's out over most of the state, there was a big accident on the Interstate, and nobody knows yet how many fishing boats were lost." He raised his camera and began snapping photos of the damaged addition. "Have they found him yet?"

"No, they're still looking," said Lucy.

"You know, I never much liked that guy," said Ted. "But I never figured him for a murderer. Shoddy construction, yes, but not murder."

"One led to the other," said Lucy. "He let the contractor substitute cheaper stuff . . ."

"And probably got a handsome kickback himself," added Bill.

"When Bitsy started comparing the invoices with the estimates she realized what he'd done, so he killed her. Then when Hayden started asking questions he got the bright idea of killing him and making it look like suicide — everyone would naturally think he was stricken with guilt and remorse for killing Bitsy. Then when he realized it was all going to come crashing down — literally — he tried to make Bill," she paused and smiled apologetically, "the fall guy."

"Can I quote you?" asked Ted, grinning wickedly.

"No!" exclaimed Lucy. "Absolutely not. I don't want to get charged with tasteless punning."

They were enjoying a shared laugh when a flurry of activity caught their attention. One of the searchers was waving to the ambulance crew that was standing by. They responded quickly, jumping out of the cab where they had been keeping warm and rushing into the wrecked building with a stretcher. It seemed like quite a while before they emerged, carrying a shrouded form. Bill and Lucy watched silently, but Ted hurried over to question the searchers.

"I can't say I'm unhappy he's dead," confessed Bill.

"Me, either," said Lucy with a little shudder. "He killed two people and he would have killed you, too, just to make some money. What was it for?"

"He wasn't the kind of guy who could ever say no — not to a supplier with a shady deal, not to a worker who found a shortcut. You can't run a business like that. Plus, he had to be a big shot — he liked living high on the hog. He had to have a big roll of bills in his pocket, he had to have the biggest truck, the hunting trips. If business wasn't good, and it hasn't been this winter because of the weather, he had to get his money somewhere else. He wasn't the kind of guy who would tighten his belt and wait for things to get better."

"I didn't like him at the board meeting but then I felt guilty when I saw him at the food pantry. I guess that was just another kind of showing off," said Lucy. "I don't think he really wanted to kill you, you know. He kept trying to warn me off — the near miss when the kids were sledding, the car fire. I guess he thought he had no choice when he saw me with that folder."

"The stupid thing is I never even looked at it. I didn't know what was going on

338

when he started to fight with me on that roof. I thought he'd lost his mind."

"I'm sure glad you're okay."

"Me, too."

Arm in arm, they turned to go and encountered Chuck Canaday.

"This is one hell of a mess," he said, shaking his head.

Then he reached out and clasped Bill's hand. "How are you feeling?"

"Just had the wind knocked out of me — thanks to the snow and my down jacket."

Canaday nodded, then his gaze shifted to the library building. He sighed and shook his head. "What a shambles. All the work and planning that went into that addition, not to mention two lives. All because he was greedy."

"Do you have any idea how much Ed took?" Lucy had to know.

"I figured it out last night. I think it was close to $50,000. It wasn't just the roof, you know. He shaved something off everything. Carpeting. Light fixtures, everything. And this was a half-million-dollar project."

"What will happen now?"

"I don't know. I can tell you one thing, though. The board has plenty of work to do." He looked at Bill. "I don't suppose I could persuade you to fill one of the vacancies?"

Bill scratched his beard. "Sorry," he said. "I'm not much of a reader."

Epilogue

*. . . and they all lived happily
ever after.*

A year later, as Lucy poured herself a cup of punch at the dedication of the newly completed Julia Ward Howe Tilley wing of the library, the awful night of the Valentine's Day blizzard had already receded into the distant past. The reconstruction had gone smoothly, and standing in the rebuilt children's room, she found it hard to believe she had stood in the snow last winter and watched it collapse into a heap of rubble.

Once again there were sparkling windows and fresh, clean carpeting; the child-sized chairs and low bookshelves had all been replaced. In addition, several computer stations now provided access to the larger world beyond Tinker's Cove. And high above them, Lucy knew, strong steel beams properly supported the roof that provided protection from rain and snow and cold.

It would all be perfect, she thought, except for one thing: Josiah's Tankard was still missing from its glass case in the vestibule.

But this was no time to dwell on the negative, thought Lucy, taking a sip of punch and looking about at the crowded library. Today was a day of celebration, and apparently nobody had wanted to miss it. In addition to the board members Lucy spotted many familiar faces: Barney had planted himself in a corner and was chewing the fat with the fire chief; Ted Stillings was snapping pictures and getting quotes for *The Pennysaver* from the librarian, Eunice Sparks; and both Edna and Edith Withers had come, enlivening the scene with their matching pink and orange plaid pantsuits. Juanita and a group of mothers had gathered in a circle, chatting and bouncing toddlers on their hips.

"Lucy, let's check out the food," invited Sue, leading the way to the buffet table. "I hear Corney has gone all out."

Lucy had to agree. The long table was filled with platters of tiny cakes and sandwiches; there were mounds of fruit topped with strawberries dipped in chocolate, and plates heaped with cookies for the children. Menus, hand written in calligraphy, were placed at each end of the table.

"This Aunt Fannie's salmon spread is pretty good," admitted Sue, peering at the menu. "I wonder where she got the recipe?"

Corney beamed at her from her spot behind the table; these days she was only too happy to share the credit. "It's in the Fannie Farmer cookbook," she crowed. "I got the idea from Lucy — she told me how she always called the book 'Aunt Fannie' because it made her feel she had a helper in the kitchen." She bent closer. "In order to settle that awful lawsuit I agreed to provide attribution for my recipes and this seemed like a charming way to do it, don't you think?"

"I guess," said Sue, reaching for another sandwich.

"There's more to creating good food than a recipe, anyway," said Lucy. "It's the ingredients you choose, and the care you take in combining them."

"I couldn't agree more," said Corney, holding out a plate. "Try these cheese puffs."

"Mmm," said Lucy, reaching for another. "Terrific. Today I'm forgetting about calories."

Noticing a buzz of activity near the

doorway, Lucy and Sue made their way through the crowd. Reaching the circulation desk, they found a pink and beaming Miss Tilley surrounded by a group of her cronies. She was waving a letter.

"I just got it today — it's from Lu Asquith — she's arranged to purchase Josiah's Tankard and is presenting it to the library!"

"But how can she do that?" asked Dot Kirwan, who was always up to date on the gossip thanks to her job at the IGA. "Last I heard, the bank was taking the house. She was going to move in with her sister in Florida until Gerald gets out of jail next year."

"She was," nodded Miss Tilley. "In fact, she was packing to go. She was going through Gerald's things, deciding what to keep and what to give away, and she found a Lotto ticket. They're good for a year, you know, so she took it to the Quik-Stop. They punched it into the machine and you know what?" Miss Tilley paused, enjoying keeping everyone in suspense. "It was worth two million dollars!"

For a moment the room was silent, then there was an explosion of voices.

"Wow," said Sue. "That's some lucky lady."

"Yeah," nodded Lucy. "But it's kind of awful in a way. Just think how different things might have been for Gerald. I wonder if he just forgot it or . . ."

Her thoughts were interrupted by the sound of a spoon tapping against a glass.

"It's time to get started," began Chuck. "I promise I won't keep you from those delicious refreshments for long. But as chairman of the library board I need to acknowledge some very hard-working people. As you all know, we suffered a terrible blow last February when the original addition collapsed. Rebuilding would not have been possible without the cooperation of the Megunticook Insurance Company, and I especially want to thank Henry Howe, the vice president in charge of claims, for his guidance and understanding."

He paused, indicating a gray-haired man in a suit, and there was a polite round of applause.

"A very big thank you is also due to librarian Eunice Sparks, who managed to keep the library up and running throughout this difficult period."

Eunice bobbed her head and was greeted with smiles and more applause.

"I also want to thank our new board

members, who weren't afraid to take on a challenge that sometimes seemed overwhelming: Juanita Orenstein, the Reverend Clive Macintosh, and Jack Mulroney from the Tinker's Cove Savings Bank."

He paused again, and there was another round of applause.

"And, of course, great thanks is due to the faithful board members who held firm and did not flee from adversity: Lucy Stone and my lovely wife, Corney Clarke Canaday, who is responsible for the wonderful refreshments we are all enjoying today."

This was met with an enthusiastic outburst of clapping and even a few whistles from the men gathered in the corner, but Chuck held up his hand, asking for quiet.

"Finally, it is time to acknowledge the person who has given the most to the library throughout the years and the person in whose honor we are dedicating this fine new addition: Miss Julia Ward Howe Tilley. To commemorate this occasion I have a plaque to present to Miss Tilley — where are you?"

There was a hush as Miss Tilley came forward, moving slowly and leaning on Rachel's arm. When she finally reached the front of the room, Chuck had to swallow hard before he could continue.

"I think everyone here agrees with me that if there is one person who exemplifies the spirit of this library, it is Miss Tilley. As the librarian for many years and then as a board member, she has always maintained that our town's most valuable assets are the inquiring minds of its residents and has insisted that the library provide the information and inspiration needed to nourish those minds. In recognition of her life-long contribution to Tinker's Cove, I hereby dedicate this new addition the Julia Ward Howe Tilley Room."

He bent down, placing the plaque in her shaking hands and planting a kiss on her cheek.

"That's something I've wanted to do for a long time," he joked, prompting the crowd to erupt in a cheerful ovation. Lucy enthusiastically joined the clapping, blinking furiously to stop the tears that were filling her eyes.

When the noise finally began to subside, Miss Tilley took a step forward.

"This is truly a wonderful honor and I want to thank you all very much," she said, clutching the plaque to her chest. "But as marvelous as all this is, I have to admit that it's not quite enough."

There was a stunned silence. Chuck looked as if he'd been slapped. "What do you mean?" he asked.

"Well," she said, taking a step forward and lifting her chin in a challenge. "The one thing that would please me more than anything would be for Tinker's Cove to have the highest per capita circulation in the state."

"That doesn't sound too hard — what would it take to do that, Eunice?"

"Every card holder would have to borrow 12 books," answered Eunice, peering over her half-glasses from her post behind the circulation desk.

"That's just one a month — we can do that, can't we, folks?"

Chuck's question was met with nods and murmurs of assent until Corney stepped forward.

"I'd like to sweeten the challenge, if I may," she said, fluttering her eyelashes coyly. "I'll be happy to bake a Marvelous Mocha Cheesecake for the person who reads the most books in one year."

"Hear that, everybody?" announced Chuck. "The person who reads the most books wins a cake!"

Corney's offer was met with great approval from the crowd, who cheered and clapped. Lucy sneaked a peek at Sue, and caught her rolling her eyes. Sue didn't seem to like the new, kinder and gentler Corney any more than she had liked the earlier, pricklier version.

"Well, I've had enough of this," she said, setting her plate down on the table and brushing off her hands. "It's time to hit the road before all this sweetness and light sends me into insulin shock."

"I ought to get going, too," said Lucy. "But first I want to congratulate Miss Tilley. See you later."

She turned, intending to join the group that had gathered around Miss Tilley, but was discouraged by the large number of people. She wouldn't be missed, she decided, resolving to stop by for a visit tomorrow. If she didn't get home and get the pot roast started soon, it wouldn't be ready in time for supper.

Leaving the group, she headed for the computers, where Zoe and Sadie were playing an educational game.

"It's time to go, Zoe. Could you please turn off the computer and say good-bye to Sadie?"

"Aw, Mom," whined the little girl, sticking out her lower lip in a pout. "Can't I play just one more game?"